Poking 360

Larry Greer

Poking around in the world's and the universe's business.

Foreword

1 - This collection of essays is a labor of love/hate pitched into by a half self-inclusive and half self-aggrandizing misanthrope of the activist and the tender and the peaceful and the mostly well-meaning variety in that he wants no harm done whatsoever to any of his brothers and sisters in the moronic top-down ranks of the worldwide labor force of human boneheads working all week long and overtime and on weekends and holidays to squander all their/our human promise as opposed to lifting a single first finger apiece to save ourselves from ourselves using a classic affiliative or even a full-blown ear-to-ear Duchenne kind of human smile and a simple and age-old friendly curling motion in the first fingers in question to invite the shell-shocked better angels of our nature to come out of hiding after all this time.

2 - In other words, you could say this book is the love/hate child of the super morally disappointed misanthropist in me and the gushy lovesick philanthropic side of myself who's head over heels for the truly beautiful beings we could all be together on paper as the saying goes.

3 - And if I do say so myself I crushed it when I chose "Poking" as the word picture worth a thousand words devoted to capturing all at once what a reader should expect from this book loaded with essays that take all kinds of pokes at humanity at large when they're not busy poking fun at or poking a finger in the chest or poking a stick in the eye of the best and brightest and highest and mightiest one's among us who also get holes poked in their claims to greatness for the oversized parts

they play in the already mentioned squandering of all our human promise.

4 - Pretty regularly the book also deeply pokes a citizen-grade philosopher of science's nose into the business of existence itself in a universe so stupidly kluged together that human consciousness or something a lot like it must be the thing pulling the strings so to speak on this overcomplicated cosmos that only grows into a more hopelessly gordian ravel the more enormously inordinate is the brainpower we pour into raveling it.

5 - The already mentioned lovesick philanthropist in me likes to think that all this poking at its core is actually a matter of poking and poking and poking the deeply sleeping gentle giant of a lovable hug-happy teddy bear we all must have in us judging by how wonderful it feels in the off moments when we're not super busy squandering all our promise as beings equipped with a love hormone for literally goodness sake and other ennobling stuff like mirror neurons and the good kind of little angel on at least one of our shoulders and the ability to feel truly beautiful things like humility and simple pleasures and to come up with a gem like the Golden Rule and let's not forget a precious thing like the inborn life instinct we ought to be able to rejuvenate enough even at this late date for it to finally override this anomic collective death wish we're getting closer to fulfilling by the minute.

6 - Of course the morally disappointed misanthrope in me is only doing all this poking out of impotent if not outright blind rage and maybe (in the spirit of full disclosure) as a way to self-aggrandizingly set himself

apart a little from the herd of human brothers and sisters out there of all ages and shapes and sizes and pronouns for making traditional and special and extra-special reference to them who've so miserably grown OK with our race going down without a fight of the noble variety as opposed to the mind-boggling and always growing array of other kinds of small and medium and large and extra-large and extra extra-large-scale varieties of fighting that are taking us all down in the first place.

7 - And finally, the so-called dear reader can expect to run sometimes into some poking around for some sort of last-ditch miracle robust enough to tuck and stuff all the awfulness poking out from behind and under and inside of everything we touch including each other back into the hole we let it crawl out of for some ugly unknown reason.

Conatus

1 - So much has been made of all the Spinozan noses and shoulders and buns and necks and nerves that respectively have been kept to the grindstone and put to the wheel and busted and broken and strained to keep respectively sinking and putting no end of teeth and backs into sparing no pains to keep sustaining the conatus that has deposited us all here at this really deep end of the salt mines that life is when we're practically slave-driven to persevere in our existence without ever forgetting to also keep enhancing the existence in question by rolling up the old sleeves and pouring untold gallons of elbow grease and blood and sweat and tears

and midnight oil into all the grunt and donkey work and all the hard yakka it takes to keep supplying the need to keep supplying the heaps and heaps of multiplying needs that come with the onus of preserving the kind of runaway way of life that unrolls when an irresistible slave-driver like nisus is at the controls as the Spinozan story goes.

2 - But what if the story is mostly or even wholly wrong and what we're calling a 24-7-365 grinding out of a more and more high-priced and desirable lifestyle is more like a coasting along on a load of momentum that's been painstakingly conserved (and maybe even more painstakingly and preternaturally augmented) since the day we threw the weight of our big Darwinian win against all other comers behind the launching of ourselves into this dogged pursuit of hard-bought and extra-Darwinian self-improvement that thanks to Newton and his first law has shot us well past the point of diminishing returns on all our toiling for the spoils so to speak of all the toiling that grows only more and more exorbitant the deeper we keep being gyro-piloted into territory where there's so precious little in the way of external forces with the juice to outdo our built-up resistance to changes in our crazy outdated state of motion?

3 - What if we're nothing but freeloaders along for the free ride of mindlessly and idly keeping ourselves occupied with all our toiling like Trojans as a way to shirk the harder work of correcting this course that keeps busy-beelining us down a growing list of onerous chores to which no one ever adds the so overdue task of grinding out a halt on all this overdoing of the so-called self-

improvement that only seems to grow more crucial the longer we keep following the no-pain-no-gain rule into the next area where it takes even more pain to gain ground on whatever it is we're not so merrily chasing into the next and the next and the next area where it keeps taking more pain to keep gaining access to the greater pains it takes to keep gaining on what we're chasing like a race of Algers of the Horatio persuasion or maybe to keep gaining heavier and heavier breathing space between us and some something that never stops giving us chase?

4 - Or what if all this making the dust fly with all this mad implacable shaking of the dust of wherever we are off our feet is a function of a funny feeling that if the dust ever settled we'd see that the real thrust of all this breakneck racing toward the offing so to speak is a succumbing to the drawing power of a long thanatotic holiday from a life instinct going so overboard as to brutally convolute this mortal coil to the point of lending no end of subliminal sweetness to the siren song of a good long thanatotic holiday from all the mounting sound and fury churned out by the age-old initial conditions that might have but didn't give and given rise anti-respectively to a not un-Edenic tendency toward the next and the next and the next better plane of plain old ordinary everyday gratefulness for life's simpler pleasures?

Margins

1 - The habitual scrutiny of the universe by the science types seems to just keep fishily drilling it all down to the tricky issue of margins like the putative lines that can be drawn between one staunch or one in and out-popping resider in spacetime and its neighbors or between all the asymptotically smaller and smaller growing fractions of the span between any given here and now and a certain suspiciously soupy moat between us and destination points like T=0 called a Planck's length or between a nearby particle separated from the partner it's entangled with by an improbable margin with no clear limits on its odd broadness or between the infinite tiny-bit different universes said by many to be needed to square the circle of explaining away the altogether undifferentiated superposition the craziest (so far) natives of spacetime are wont to go and get themselves lost in when they go unwatched.

2 - And of course there are also the odd margins between a mind and an animate and a body and an inanimate thing, respectively and then there's the fine line between touchable stuff like matter and its airier Siamese twin-like brother or sister going by the name of energy and also the maybe even finer if not even the downright iffy line between the thing that can become or not become of a cat when it's placed out of sight if not mind for a while by a science type who's designed a 50-50 chance of killing it in the name of science and there's maybe even the iffier line between the points in space and time on either side of the arrival of a property of the probably emergent variety like consciousness that's come to cross

some odd threshold between us and its starting point somewhere and somewhen out there in the cosmos and finally let's not leave out the gossamer margin where the quantum realm and its less infinitesimal and also more ordinary counterpart are said to come together or whatever in the world there is that could possibly be separating the Big Bang from the moment before detonation.

3 - "Bourn" is a ridiculously good word for employing in the sorting out of the issues continuously dividing the ones partial to the particles born so to speak of the pointillistic point of view and the seconders of the oneness that is so well represented by so emblematically undiscontinuous a thing as the stream that bourn is a synonym of as opposed to its synonymical affiliations with such almost diametrical opposites of a flowing so-called body as a boundary and as a domain that can't even be conceived of without a supposititious thing like a boundary and as a goal or objective that can't very well kind of materialize out there on an oddly marginy thing called a horizon without a setup where there are bourns galore to be proverbially crossed when gotten to on the way to the bourn in question and this is all to say nothing of the explosion of double and often opposite meanings that is touched off when bourn's homonymical affiliations with the words "born" and "borne" are taken fully into consideration and nor is it to say anything about the possibility of tapping so wholly into the koanic value of dwelling on a word stuffed like bourn is with paradoxical possibilities that one's life winds up paradoxically dividing in a flash of enlightenment into a before and an after the indiscreet sweeping of discreteness sweetly out of the literally whole equation.

4 - Similarly Parmenides of Elea is a good name for dropping when it comes to ontologically mediating between the all-is-one bunch and the bunch bunch who buy it when their own four eyes tell them that reality is founded on the very chunks of discontinuity that led Parmenides a couple of millenniums ago and change to raise the troublesome matter of what stuff other than chunks of discontinuity is supposed to be making its home in the problematical manner of cranny that really has to be a thing for one chunk of discontinuity to stand out from and not singularly or maybe unsingularly blend with all the others.

5 - Likewise a certain Eleatic School's star pupil going (without the actual getting of anywhere as per his own paradoxes) by the name of Zeno can help us move the needle (minus that thing about moving) on this mattery issue with his having proved many times over that the fact of the matter is there's no such thing as moving through a putative medium like the time and space between, say, an archer and her or his target when the medium in question can be hacked from larger to smaller and ever smaller fractions of itself all the way down to the very good point that infinite divisibility actually means there's no such thing as the divisibility needed to shoot down Parmenides' ultimately positionless position that all is one and vice versa (if that way of saying it doesn't throw a chunk of discontinuity called a monkey wrench in the works of the whole oneness thing).

6 - All the above of which brings us back around to a certain awesome godsend for the bunch called the Planck length where so many arguments for the oneness of it all

go to die even though its reputation as a base unit is shot through with holes big enough for an admittedly tiny person to drive a semitruck-load of questions through like how on earth could it be that Zeno's arrow can get to a there and a then from a here and a now, respectively after all thanks to an incredibly elfin stretch of the most impenetrable nebulousness ever and how could it be that the bunch bunch are so OK with this super fun-size occasion for taking the kinds of two-footed leaps of blind faith normally associated with the ones who zealously jump at occasions to level tits and tats at the four-eyed and pointy-headed and holier-than-thou science types for leveling tats and tits at them, respectively for the faith-based nature of their relationship with all god's creation as they say.

7 - Seriously though, how on earth could a murky little curtain obscuring god knows what way down there somewhere be all it takes to spell curtains for the oneness bunch's sureness that our ingrained blind faith in what our respective sets of two and four eyes keep telling us about the grainy nature of this existence is misplaced in that all our amazing compliments of blind faith ought to be saved for sticking religiously to the lead-pipe cinch that byproducts of granularity like lead pipes are aught but particularly die-hard crotchets brought about by all the grains and grains of salt that go untaken with the assurances from the bunch bunch that there's no need to look behind a certain curtain of murkiness for insights into why in the world so many grains and grains of untruth have been inserted into the works of the wooden-headedness it takes to keep forging full steam ahead against the grain with respect to the relentlessly trending sense that all the hemming and all the hedging

it takes to hem out the good points of the oneness bunch has hemmed the bunch bunch into a frame of mind bordering more and more on a position fringier than the one exclusively featuring the weirdness of one big barrel of fringelessness minus the barrel?

8 - Speaking of which, it sure seems like lately every so-called thing's been barrelessly barreling in truly seamless unison toward an appointment with an illusory point in spacetime wherewhen the scrutinizing of the bunch bunch's universe has become truly scrupulous enough to yield a critical massless mass's worth of all the clues and proofs out the wazoo out there pointing to the pointlessness of hewing to the pointillistic view that our only problem ontology-wise is that some kidney of hew-happy cosmic trickster figure keeps keeping one step ahead of the science types madly using the illusion of discontinuity for kluging together a more and more confusing worldview that literally includes every kind of line imaginable but the bottom line that the line of ontological thought that keeps running us into bunches of nutty whatsits is nothing really but a bunch of bologna minus the bologna and also minus the bunch and thereby minus the minus.

Lightbulb

1 - Safely shield your mind's eye and then count to three and after that with all your amazing brainpower imagine the awesome luminosity that would probably wash everything out if a 100 or even a 50 or a 25 watt lightbulb actually went on over billions of human heads at the same time that super coincidentally it simultaneously popped into all the Darwinianly well-formed heads in question that we've been busy screwing the pooch with respect to how we've been using the amazing *Homo sapiens* brainpower that has propelled us through the three hundred millenniums we've spent never getting to a place where we both came across and acted on the thought of doing something better with our amazing brainpower than conjure up an ever-widening variety of ways to set ourselves apart from one another.

2 - According to some crack team of us with especially crazy amounts of brainpower to burn our amazing brains are wont to process upwards of 70,000 thoughts per day day in and day out and probably have been wont to do so over most of the whole course of all those already mentioned millenniums that have seen no fewer than 117 billion of us come and then go after spending a whole human lifetime cranking out thoughts by the numberless buttload for adding to the gobsmacking number of them our race has whipped into existence since that fateful day so long ago that into the relatively capacious cranium of the first one of us popped the thought of setting him or herself apart from all the eponymously erect brothers and sisters who for their part had famously set themselves apart from all the *Homo* brothers and sisters

of the *heidelbergensis* persuasion who for their part had long since set themselves apart from an earlier genus of knuckle draggers who'd long since set themselves apart from an earlier one and so on.

3 - All of which begs a present-day *Homo sapiens* brain to give a thought or two to the good question of how many total thoughts do you get when you multiply the 70,000 daily thoughts in question times 117 billion and madly counting times an average lifetime of let's say 40 years and growing over the whole course of this long slog toward the day one of us first sets her or himself apart from the outdated dipshit *H. sapiens.*

4 - And over the course of piling up that higher than sky-high number of thoughts how many times did it happen that one of us thought to wonder why on earth we went to all the trouble to evolve as one into the same race only to turn around and bring about a certain misnomer called civilization that's little more than an organized subjecting of ourselves for some unknown reason to record numbers of occasions for estrangement from one another (and all the awfulness that comes with it) on tribal and hierarchical and gender and sociopathological and a mind-boggling variety of other kinds of grounds?

5 - It makes a person want to cry like a baby at the thought of a race of orphaned little brainchildren out there spawned by the ones of us who have thought about how to stop using all our awesome brainpower so miserably and then never bothered to fend for the sweet little nippers or organize a village for doing so no matter

how much more awful and voluminous and also ominous have become the cognitive spawn of all the mama bear-like tiger moms on all sides of all the growing number of gender and other kinds of divides clawing away at the very last layers of our protections against the suicidal anomie we could so easily beat if we used a healthy amount of our amazing collective brainpower all at once to imagine what life would be like if we were all united by the thought that the enemy to be rallied together against here in what's looking more and more like the 11th hour is all of us with all our idiotic die-hard fondness for all this ridiculous division.

Time

1 - Maybe the best thing about the mulish illusion of Time is that it allows us to track how wrong our best and brightest keep being in all their scientific findings and all their educated guesswork and their deductions and their hunches about what's what in every specialty and other kind of area under the sun including the study of Time itself and also the Space that got attached to it as just one (though admittedly pretty big) example of our best guesstimaters making up for the wrong way to look at a subject of study that replaced the wrong way to look at it that had replaced the earlier wrong way to look at it that had replaced an earlier one and so on.

2 - The changes in states that our wrong conception of Time either seems to make possible or seems to be

roughly or exactly equivalent to make it edifying child's play to follow the sky-high rise of the human pyramid's worth of our species' generations literally upon generations of geniuses making giants out of themselves time and time again if you will by changing minds about how right the giants on whose shoulders they're standing were when it was their turn to be wrong about what's what out there in a putatively real universe with what seems to be a bottomless supply of ways to make the Einsteins go wrong in their thinking about what existence is.

3 - And this is to say nothing about how wrong the soft-scientific equivalents of the rocket scientists and how wrong the citizen equivalents of this soft variety of eggheads keep getting it in their formulating of the ways we're all supposed to think about the coexistence we never get any closer to getting right for all the mental elbow grease the thought leaders keep pouring into the working out of such super user-friendly game plans for relating to one another as the ones laying out the array of social hierarchies of the manorial persuasion and the seignorial and of course the royal and the feudal and the monarchial absolutist and the theocratic and the socialistic and capitalistic of the authoritative and of the oligarchic and corporate and plutocratic and vulture and unfetteredly free and neoliberal variety, respectively.

4 - And let's not not mention this illusion of Father Time's help in spawning a long lineup of such accessory institutions and figures and symbols as chattel and bonded and this modern-day child sex ilk of slavery and colonialization and imperialism and the super Great

Chain of Being and the social stripe of Darwinism and demigodliness and untouchableness and of course the notion of overmanhood and all things Randian and a good old boy going by the name of *Homo economicus* and way too many kinds of modern-day tribalism to name especially when you consider how many more kinds would have been added to the mix in the course of trying to name the crush of furiously worked-up ones that already existed.

5 - Perhaps it's time if you will for all us self-glorified seekers of knowledge to start beating ourselves up for completely missing the hint that Time doesn't really exist that's pretty glaringly inherent in the unchanging fact that the more things keep changing the more they keep staying the same with all us ill-qualified knowledge seekers so timelessly proving unequal to such basic cognitive tasks as learning to know better than to never stop never self-correcting when we keep getting it wrong in choosing between equality and its opposite in laying the foundation for how members of the very same human race go about getting along.

The Spectrum

1 - Perhaps now that we've entered an era where in various settings we formally share where we are on the gender spectrum (unless we're one of those who's taken the leap all the way off of one end of it or the other) perhaps we should ask ourselves if there are maybe other features of our respective beings that we should be announcing out loud by now by way of letting all the so-called others with respect to us know how best to think about and treat us in our dealings with each other as we go about this business of briskly separating ourselves from the underdeveloped social creatures we were before some new tool like for instance gender declaring or maybe like an incredibly even lengthier social extension ladder got tossed into the mix of civilization.

2 - Speaking of which maybe the next characteristic we should be revealing at our in-person and our virtual get-togethers is our personal score on the self-importance scale we of course would first need to precisely codify so we'd all be ironically seeing eye to eye when it came to visualizing how much higher or lower one do-gooding reporter of her or his or their (not by a long shot meant to be an exhaustive list) self-importance score is on the scale than another.

3 - Perhaps a wide-ranging and multiplied mixed-sex and mixed-gender team of USDA beef graders and private-enterprise skyscraper and or mineshaft makers and a lot of top-notch taxonomists of various stripes and feathers and some of the best and brightest American Kennel Club

judges on earth and a semi-cross-disciplinary A-team's worth of anthropological science types of the cultural and the social and the sociocultural and maybe also the biological and the biocultural and the political and the economic and the psychological and the politico-economico-psychologico and the paleo and the ethnoarcheological variety could start at the far lowest end of the in-progress spectrum in question and hammer out the wording if you will for nailing down the lower numbers of designations on a 100-point scale with the help of an ethnographic battery of question and answer sessions perhaps with such low self-importance individuals as the constant butts of the brutal belittling that accrues to an aspiring mighty hunter when at the bare feet of his half-naked Old World hunter-gatherer clan he drops another sumptuous proof of the superior hunting prowess that would render him too big for the britches he's not even wearing if the village it took to raise him (minus that thing about rising) didn't keep helping him keep his bare feet on the ground so he could be easily reached when it came time again for the village to knock the toxic pridefulness out of him.

4 - If dipping all the way back into the Old World is too much trouble the team could also just pick the brain maybe of some Newer World low self-importance individual like a third-world war casualty's newly bereaved mother or father who's been blown from a worn-out arm or rocking chair in her or his humble family home all the way up to the heights of grief and has thereby usefully reached a viewpoint for having a good enough look at the proverbial grand scheme of things to have interesting things to say to the team about how much less self-importance we all could use in these first

and second and third worlds where so many big and littler villages are lying down on the job of repeatedly knocking the most pridefully self-important ones down to size so they stop rising up and running the whole shit show that keeps getting the sons and daughters of less important people maimed and killed when it's not busy maiming and killing the less important mothers and fathers of the sons and daughters in question themselves when it's not busy doing both things at once plus a lot of other nasty stuff in the horrible sorting out of who gets the bragging rights self-importance-wise.

5 - On second thought we might need a thousand or maybe a million-point or even a madly upward sliding self-importance scale in light of how miserably all the New World villages have long been failing to install the ceilings on their social structures that might spare them the ever more virulent and flood-like trickle-down toxicity of the sky-high self-importance individuals.

6 - Speaking of which, let's go all the way back down for a minute to the lowest-most end of our speculative self-importance index and think about how worthwhile it would be for our all-star team of scale makers to get the perspective of the growing coffle's worth of dead men and women wading through the rising pools of awful toxicity that have trickled in floods all the way down to the floors of the unceilinged social structures piling up the deaths of despair you get in nothing but clusters when the lowest self-importance individuals in the villages with high self-importance individuals in them reach the point where they are in unimportance

"Stepped in so far, that, should [they] wade no more/Returning were as tedious as go o'er."

7 - At any rate, getting back to the fountainheads of all this trickling down, our world-class ethnographic field team of brainpickers are certain to find that these founts and all their almost as self-important rainmakers and other kinds of high-end members of the villages' anti-ceiling (and anti-floor) leagues are more than eager (as in a deadly tidal bore) wellsprings of downpouring pennies from heaven in the form of the two cents' worth put in many many times over when it comes to one of these high-enders covering the grounds for keeping ceilings off the social structures so newer and newer heights can always be reached by the highest self-importance individuals a society really really needs if it plans to have the most penetrating pennies from heaven keep raining down by the jackpot on the lower self-importance individuals from above.

8 - Perhaps what will even turn up if our team sits down with the ones among us (minus that thing about being among us) who will characteristically gobble up all the highest numbers on the index in question is a formula for assigning the highest numbers that is so plain and simple as to be no more than a matter of adding up how many of the lower self-importance individuals a given high-end designee-in-waiting is ready to do a number on in the self-interest of personally getting to even higher numbers that involve doing an even worse number on a growing number of one's contemporaries and also on the ones who have yet to be born for having a worse and

worse number done on them by the highest self-importance individuals.

9 - So anyway, after the last of the bugs is worked out of a process for letting everybody know precisely where they stand relative to everybody else self-importance-wise all our big and littler villages could contribute a special delegate or two for joining a task force charged with whipping up a system for facilitating the quick and simple getting of everybody's respective cards on all the conference tables out there with respect to the question of which subcategory of humanity all the people with a proverbial place at any given table feel the deepest fealty to.

10 - And speaking of cards, perhaps one and all could simply carry around a card that readily identifies which one of all the growing number of human splinter groups they most tribally identify with or maybe uniforms could even come into play or baseball caps with highly personalized logos on the front panels of them or lapel pins maybe or a finer and finer slicing of the primary colors into enough shades and shades of shades and so on for each and every gang's worth of us to have our own special hue to hew to at all costs.

Rocks

1 - I truly think it's time for the International Union of Geological Science Types to finish up this seismic shift if you will into officially admitting that *H. sapiens* has thoroughly whipped Mothers Nature and Earth in our battle with them for the victor's quill for scribbling out what's left of Earth's history after the 4.543 billion years' worth of it and counting it's taken to arrive here at the very doorstep of a period to be officially christened the Anthropocene the minute our alpha rock hounds have nosed out the requisite amount of humanity's fingerprints smudging the dermises Mother Earth has spent so many epochs building up layers literally upon layers of only to be left defenseless against the mad handsy-ness of a certain proliferation of mere terrible infants when looked at in the light of the International Geological Time Scale that we ourselves devised.

2 - Now that it's all over but the shouting at each other over how on Earth to go about pulling and flipping and spinning and twisting and pushing or pressing all the levers and switches and dials and knobs and buttons, respectively on Earth's somewhat complicated systems and subsystems and systems and subsystems within systems and subsystems of a living and or an unliving and or a combinational and or an equivocal nature perhaps we earthshaking Earth history makers with the capacity for sort of metamorphically aggregating such gems as the word "chronostratigraphic" should think about exploiting our weakness for sticking our noses into the business of Earth's workings by mining the mother lode of prospective disciplines for drilling down into

knowledge of a bedrock vein in search of some kind of state-of-the-art composite like a "psychoneopetrologic" rock hard science with the mission of drilling down into all the untold strata of rocks we *H. sapiens* must have in our individual and collective heads for us to have done what we've done to Mothers Nature and Earth when we haven't been super busy laying the groundwork for doing even worse things to the two perfectly innocent sisters.

3 - Perhaps the main article of faith among the not un-Jungian new-age rock hobbyists in charge of such a cross-bred subject area could be that you can take the *H. sapiens* out of the Stone Age but you can't take the Stone Age out of a bunch of *H. sapiens* making rock stars out of themselves if you will in this idiotically ongoing Petrolithic Period spent using the Mother Sisters' own materials against them in the relegating of them to the far back seat of this Anthropocenic one-way roadtrip we're basically taking to rock bottom in a gas guzzler some sort of lead-foot's been sleeping like a rock at the wheel of so to speak.

4 - What manner of deep psychological rock layer is analogous to the layers of fossil fuel we're tapping into like there's no tomorrow if you will to keep extending this vacation further and further away from our no-brainer obligation to be smarter at the very least than a box of rocks about how we act on the hard (and also soft) scientifically gathered information that we're being dumber than a box of rocks about how we're using our borrowed individual and collective and also theoretically shared time on this Earth?

5 - Is it thanks to some internal breed or species of seepage or oozing or some strain of percolation or some other order of up-bubbling or maybe some more take-charge sort of psychological process akin to strip mining maybe or fracking or cable or directional or electro or rotary or dual-wall reverse-circulation drilling and drilling and drilling and drilling and drilling, respectively or some other form of boring that we remain awash in this bore (as in a deadly tidal flood) of crude brain fuel we're using to keep atavistically proceeding down the oily slope of this weird Darwinian outdoing of Mother Earth no matter how clearly that whole survival of the fittest gig has shifted into a drive with the death wish written all over it?

An open letter to Richard V. Reeves, the senior fellow at the Brookings Institution who wrote *Of Boys and Men, Why the Modern Male Is Struggling, Why it Matters, and What To Do About it.*

Dear Richard,

It's heartbreaking all the evidence of humanity's sad haplessness you packed into *Of Boys and Men* as you showcased all the new crosses the title characters have been left to bear next to and among all the hard rows that girls and women have been left to hoe for so long.

It's so piteous to think of our vaunted human progress taking us to yet another place where the toeholds in our current systems of coexistence keep growing iffier and iffier for some while for others they get only more inextricable (no matter how inimical the systems keep being to everyone and their mother along this so-called march of human progress).

The only way the book could have been more gut-wrenching in relation to the state of our present-day boys and men is if it hadn't left so unquestioned the conventional wisdom that boys and men had it so great back in the day when they were so solidly ensconced in the systems of coexistence that did such a number of numbers on the girls and women when they weren't busy chewing up and spitting out some boys and men so that others could knock themselves out proving themselves to be better than the ones being chewed up and spit out.

When the conventional wisdom in question is questioned it seems the boys and men can't win for losing in the hash we keep making of our human cohabitation on this planet we're now also chewing up and spitting out and doing no end of numbers on in the name of all this human progress that's now being so much better to the girls and women of the species as per a pearl of conventional wisdom the book also doesn't question.

Going back to the slacking new subspecies of human males, perhaps what's happened is that a whole band of humanity has finally had it with shouldering the onus to go out there and beat out the next onus shoulderer in adding and adding and then adding some more to all the sound and all the fury that this mortal coil amounts to when human progress is measured by how many new and improved ways we can dream up for some of us to outdo the others.

Maybe after all those so-called glory days of the male the Y chromosomes of the couches full of loafers the book is so worried about are simply on empty with respect to the right stuff it takes to keep racing for all one's worth into the crazy-making fray in the name of not getting shamefully drubbed in the go-go zero or negative-sum game of getting ahead of the next guy or gal.

When it comes to the girls and the women, the book could have been even more gut-wrenching had it not failed to factor in the sad fact that two-thirds of the girls said to be thriving circles around the lotus-eating boys are feeling chewed up and spit out emotionally as they shoulder more and more of the onus to go out there and make up for lost time spent in the back seat instead of at the wheel of all this racing faster and faster around and around in circles without ever reaching the thing we're madly chasing after or losing the thing that's madly chasing after us.

This is all not to say that the book doesn't offer a little glimmer of hope, which it does--in the form of the off chance that all this opting out of the fray on the part of the boys is a long overdue sign that our race is finally beginning to evolve beyond all the outdated Darwinian ways we human brothers and sisters have kept relating to one another for some dumb unknown reason.

Weeds

1 - I double or even triple dare the science types out there to use their mad skills at scrutiny to take a good hard look at their super hectic schedules full of more and more reconditely scrutinizing the daylights out of nature and find a day or even an afternoon or a lunch hour or a coffee or potty break for trading in their proverbial four eyes for a fresh set of two eyes unbiased by science (or the philosophy thereof) so they can take an outsider's look at the thousands and thousands of years of scientific history without being so impressedly deafened by all the earthshaking "Eureka!" moments that they can't hear themselves duly deducing in that vaunted scientific way of theirs that maybe they've been so purblinded by all those higher and higher-wattaged lightbulb flashes of brilliance that have gone on over the long procession of proverbially pointy and long-tressed heads that are said with the brighter and brighter lightbulbs over them in question to be shining the way along the road to the holy grail of the whole picture that they're missing something super important like all the hard and soft and in-between evidence everywhere that some hardly definable puckish

something or other out there has been impishly fiddling all along with all the squinty-eyed human scrutinizing of the universe by hiding in plain four-eyed sight all the overstuffed cosmos-load of not unparticle-like dots that when connected add up to the bigger picture that apparently has to be laically painted for the science types before they can see with their own two already mentioned borrowed eyes that they'll always be a step behind the also already mentioned little devil out there making sure that the whole story with respect to what in the world is up with the natural world is one of those neverending ones with a plot that gets nothing but thicker and thicker with all kinds of multiplying complications even though it's almost certainly fabricated from the whole cloth of the pure and simple and apparently blissful oneness that makes the *Unus Mundus* go round.

2 - Put another way, I invite if not defy the best and brightest of the boffins to stand on the shoulders of another one of our brand-new Anthropocene Era's science giants who is him or herself standing perhaps on the shoulders of another one of the giants in question so the hopefully light-boned but also tall and long-necked boffin up there on top is in a position to take a peek up over all the ever thickening and always taller-growing proverbial weeds the standouts in their fields keep finding themselves more and more deeply lost in as they follow the tendril-like threads of their runaway reconditeness into the patches within patches of weeds they can't see for the already mentioned threads putting the capital mental in all this filamental tangling up of the madly ramifying quest for the happy ending of all this scientific questing making the crazy invasive Japanese

knotweed look like a shrinking violet as it (the questing) heads the questers in question toward the less and less penetrable places where it will take stacks of four and five and six and more and more science giants to reach an occasion to sneak a peek at the coming wall of weeds growing taller and taller all the way to the offing it's blotting out so ominously.

3 - Side Note Number 1: As per the science types' own Richardson Effect, the more and more acutely an expert observer of the world cinches down her or his minute scrutinizing of one of its features the closer to wildly unlimited becomes the extent of the feature in question so that, for example, if the ruler used to measure the border between two potential goers to horrible war with one another called countries was some vanishingly small fraction of an inch (or a millimeter in boffinese) long the amount of perilous butting up against each other that the two potential goers to horrible war with each other called countries in question did would become near infinite and thereby very nicely offer perhaps some scientific insight into why the civilians relative to the science types like to use the awful byproducts (and also many many of the straight-up products) of the scientific enterprise in the terribly inhuman ways they do.

4 - Side Note Number 2: Kudos are probably also owed to the undertakers of the scientific enterprise in question for the especially enlightening way they represent humanity's penchant in all its various areas of endeavoring for never really getting anywhere along this march of human progress unless you count getting relentlessly to the next and the next and the next world

record's worth of unexplainable vainglory (I'm looking at you, Steven Pinker and company) over adding more snarls to an otherwise auspicious proposition like living simply and peacefully in the spirit of the *Unus Mundus*.

Hokey Pokey

1 - Boy oh boy, you read these days about uplifting stuff like William H. McNeill's thoughts on the euphoric sense of human connection that comes with a bunch of us "muscle bonding" by simply moving our bodies and their various similar appendages and other like kinds of parts in the same way at the same time in the same place to the beat of the same drummer and it makes you wonder if even here in the grips of all this suicidal anomie and other strains of malaise humanity isn't maybe just one big unanimous ultramarathon-strength line dance (of the electric or the cha cha slide persuasion maybe or the wobble or the cupid or watermelon shuffle or crawl, respectively or of course the macarena or even the boot scootin' boogie or the hoedown throwdown) away from reaching a place where in one big collective endorphin rush we can put our heads together and work out something much much better for ourselves than this awful chaotic double-time march of human progress (to the beats of who even knows how many different dumbass drummers) into the grips of all this suicidal anomie and other strains of malaise.

2 - At this point it really doesn't seem like it could hurt for us all to chicken dance or hokey pokey the night and then the day away together and then repeat it all a couple

of straight times (while keeping properly hydrated of course, perhaps in exact unison and with the same arm and same hand) on the off chance that all the long synchronizing of our dialed-in movements might, as William H. McNeill suspected it does, become deeply automatic enough for us to tap into our most fundamental uncorrupted human rhythms in traveling all the way back as one to our respective wombs where we all moved to the heartbeat of the human being we were so integrally connected to that feeling that connection again on a shared and regular basis (thanks to nothing more complicated, say, than putting your left hand in and taking your left hand out and putting your left hand in again and shaking it all about along with everybody else) might make us feel truly human enough for long enough for us to spend the nights and the days between our group dance sessions (or even maybe some easily repeatable marching band routines) eschewing some or all of the inhuman ways we keep treating one another.

3 - Maybe even as we speak our species is in the process of touching off a population-size spontaneous flash mob roughly along the lines of the Dancing Plague of 1518 (and some other years thereafter) that mass hysterically swept for a couple of months over a little Alsatian corner of the so-called Holy Roman Empire when, according to one theory, the terrible stresses of day to day life in the local Renaissance society became so great as to bring on an utter hunger for the comfort of muscle bonding that exploded into a deadly psychogenic movement disorder that spread in a perfectly natural epidemic pattern that perhaps offered the manic dancers the sort of euphoric connection with others to be gained from a highly

prescribed canario, say, or a galliard or a good old fashioned peasant wedding dance along the lines of what Breughel might have immortalized.

4 - At the very least, if such a runaway happiness in the feet overcame all of us at once for a spell so to speak, we'd finally all get a much-needed break from this deadly relentless mass-hysterical march of human progress that does nothing but keep heading into territory where the healthy and widespread kind of human connection grows only harder and harder to come by.

Human Chronome

1 - Every single spin along our spin around our local star ushers in another roughly 190 billion hours' worth of human activity (a figure that includes the strange inhuman strain of the activity in question) at this point in our 300,000-year-old population explosion that very very slowly at first and then exponentially started giving crazy rise almost overnight to the nuclear explosion's worth of ways to go wrong in our riding along on this spinning spin around the big giver of life to us all for better or worse and also for the time being.

2 - This prodigious and ever surging blitz of activity is unleashed, that is, in every single instance of some location on the equator like Quito, say, or Bogota or Nairobi zipping at literally one thousand miles per hour

right back around to where it started by the time another one of Mother Earth's rotations is done going undergone so the next one can escort the location in question (plus all its denizens and the unsafe first-world visitors who hubristically didn't listen to the international safety warnings) along its 24,000-mile promenade to its original starting point all over again at Mach one point almost five like Mother Earth was in a super big hurry to get another day over with in her stint as the lucky heavenly body in all the cosmos that the *H. sapiens* came to call home even as we've gone about the business of catastrophically overstaying the welcome showing so many growing signs of being unceremoniously (if you don't count whatever ceremony might be inherent in an apocalypse) dis-extended to us the longer the hundreds of billions of hours' worth of human and inhuman activity and counting we pack into each and every 24-hour day goes without including more than just a relatively few measly human hours all tolled devoted to reclaiming the old glacial and saner pace that gave our kind time to scratch our heads full of growing underused brainpower and scratch our once inhumanly hirsute butts and maybe rub our sculpted chins a little and furrow our once beetled brows while thinking twice or maybe even more times than that about adopting the already mentioned ways to go wrong we keep stupidly accumulating and never ever jettisoning on our march of human progress toward the door on this home we're so set on being shown for some dumb unknown reason.

3 - It makes you want to engage for a minute in the new human activity of wondering if our zipping around and around at one and a half times the speed of sound or so has meant somehow that we can't ever be reached by the

sound of some helpful cosmic alarm going off or by the music of the spheres as it builds and builds toward a horror-show crescendo's worth of fair and scary warning that some much badder shit (much much badder) than usual's about to happen or by the almighty tsk tsks and the tut tuts of the gods and goddesses we've populated the heavens with or by the snickers of the more malevolent entities we've not un-similarly projected into the netherly areas or by the hideous lip-licking of the abominable cosmic maw in charge of so altogether disappearing existence's biggest idiots that it's like they were never here to pull such dumbshit stunts as never choosing to stop growing into nothing but bigger and bigger idiots as one of their signature activities.

4 - And now thanks to the Human Chronome Project one of the human activities being pitched into while unsafe equatorial locations like Kinshasa and Guayaquil and Rio de Janeiro are racing back to the same unsafe place where they started is the scientific quantifying of what tends to go on in one of the twenty-six thousand and two-hundred and eighty 24-hour periods that make up the average human compliment of hours spent adding day by day to the bazillion hours' worth of the cumulative global human and inhuman activity that piles up over the course of an average one of us making our way from cradle to grave without ever engaging in nearly enough of the individual and collective activities it would take to change the nature of our dumbshit signature activities.

5 - Speaking of which, to our daily routines perhaps we should all try finding a little room for adding the human activity of hoping that the poor science types connecting

the data points in producing a big picture of the use we're daily making of the hours we have left on this planet are getting the therapy and other kinds of help they need to make it all the way to the end of their natural or god-given compliment of lifetime hours as opposed to forgoing a bunch of them owing to the desolating effects of totaling up all the untold global human hours devoted to such mortifying group activities as everybody around the globe waking up in their respective mornings rearing to put in another good hard day's work in the slog toward shattering the last decade's record of doubling the depression rates of the species' teenagers.

6 - And then of course there's the demoralizing scientific quantification of all the hours in a day we each spend turning a blind and a deaf eye and ear, respectively to such plain and simple facts of human life as the no-brainer that relentlessly devoting so many waking and other kinds of hours to arranging ourselves in dumbass top-down social structures like a certain age-old monument to top-downness called the slave-built pyramid is nothing but a great way to enable the least human and most toxically self-important examples of humanity to spend all hours of each and every day and night abusing the power over their fellow human beings that's sure enough corrupted them as per the hard and fast and ever unbending much less broken rule we've all long known about without ever managing to act like we do by reducing the stupid amounts of power over others the most inhuman and toxically self-important ones among us can just keep accumulating more and more of because the lower-down commonality can't ever find room in their hectic pathetic schedules to engage together in the daily human activity of building and

maintaining the much needed hard ceilings that would close our species off from the godawful places that runaway upward social mobility takes the so-called elite of our species.

7 - If we can't get around to getting the big prosocial stuff done like building the hard ceilings in question (or the hard floors of course) at least maybe we can find the time in our already mentioned pathetic schedules to briefly appease the miffed gods and goddesses (on whose pearly doors our elite are knocking louder and louder on by the day) by saying a quick little prayer at maybe even a veteran prayer-patterer's blazing pace and while multi-taskingly engaged in one or more of the dumbass activities in our usual daily routine in the hope that some small favor on our behalf might be divinely extended to the ones who are unluckier even than us like the well-established clusters of our brothers and sisters headed for deaths of despair and like some new potential clusters like the poor science types out there right now painstakingly subjecting themselves to the soul-crushing spectacle of all us selfie-snapping patters of ourselves on the back and all the throwers of ourselves into the virtual rounds of applause and the standing O's for ourselves organized by the elite of our species so enough of us keep being button-bustingly proud of the awful garbage that shoots out of the systems of coexistence we keep pouring nothing but more and more narcissistic and otherwise toxically self-interested garbage into.

Trains of Thought

1 - There ought to be a box with a slot built into it for the public to tuck some handwritten suggestions into as a tried and true way for us to feel included as the species' thought and also deed leaders pitch us all into the slew of enterprises of great pith and great moment that never don't get carried through because the native hue of our fearless leaders' resolution ne'er gets sicklied o'er by the pale cast of a second thought and the leaders in question are ne'er e'er bothered by the conscience that does make cowards of us all if you don't count the ones with too small a human compliment of conscience to bat an eye even when it comes to pitching us all into such Brave New World kinds of enterprises as the soaring to newer and ever newer and more dizzying heights in the putting of crazy alienating distance between the ones at the top like the fearless thought and deed leaders and the ones on the ground floor and in the basement and in the parking area of this skyscraping social structure virtually featuring a horizontal continent's-worth of vertically organized zip and area codes to go with the arrangement of better and better and more and more coveted and worse and worse and less and less coveted neighborhoods depending on whether one's headed in the up or the down direction, respectively.

2 - The almost conscience-free denizens of the penthouse suites atop the edifice in question don't so much as gulp even once before launching into the next next-level campaign to keep carrying through on the long ongoing pith and moment-loaded private enterprise of allowing no steam to speak of to build from the floors below when

it comes to public enterprises like undermining the ongoing meteoric rise of the fearless leaders by building up the already-mentioned steam needed to carry through on the enterprise of avoiding the social and the planetary catastrophe to end all catastrophes that most if not all our vaunted human enterprises of the greater and greater pith and moment variety have so long and so plainly been forming out there in the offing that you really have to wonder what the general public was thinking in its allowing the thought and deed leaders of the species to be the kinds of people who need to socially climb and climb and climb till they virtually reach a bird's eye view of the curvature of the world they're setting on fire as the saying goes and then when they get there and see the apocalypse on the horizon decide to just keep climbing and climbing and climbing higher and higher by way of the same suicidal and also homicidal human enterprises like wars of the class and many many other varieties.

3 - It also makes you think about the prospective next generation of thought and perhaps deed (or misdeed) leaders called the machine learners our current thought and (mis)deed leaders of the biological variety are madly populating the already Brave New World with without batting an eye or providing a suggestion box or a suggestion inbox so the general biological public and all the less precocious members of this generation of once innocent little machine learners, respectively don't feel completely left out of the loop in all this second-thought-free capitalizing on how much higher and higher for a while an upper class-worth of biological thought and (mis)deed leaders can keep rising when they go unbothered by the quantity of conscience it would take

for them to stop all this double-time marching of us all into one common offing that grows only darker and darker with awfulness the nigher draws the time when the Sun comes around and tries to shine on the day when the thought and (mis)deed leaders of the machine variety become even better than their biological predecessors at rising to the ever rising top to the terrible detriment of everything and everybody below.

4 - This terrified member of the general public would gladly stand in even the longest and most slow-moving of lines during some kind of public comment period designed to make me feel included in the enterprise of subjecting ourselves to the artificially conjured next level of our so already mind-bogglingly nocuous human intelligence by giving me a minute at the microphone after I've soaked up the people power that surely would come with communing in a long and windy queue with my peers of the biological variety and also with all my machine-learning cousins lucky enough to come with wheels included or the ability to hover like a drone maybe (or with the help of some kind of military-grade breakthrough in anti-gravity technology) or the knack for approximating a human or a worm-like crawl or a snake-like slither or a walk of the four or even the two-legged persuasion or maybe with the ability to pull off the sportier and even more notable trick of operating a pogo stick.

5 - And sure, it would be a little hard to know where to start when I finally got to the microphone in question, but I like to think that even without my boasting the so extraordinary number of IQ points and all the poise the

thought leaders have to play with, I would manage even under all the stress of public speaking to think of stuff like clearing my throat and then maybe hemming once or twice and or hawing and then pretending to be a little verklempt (if I wasn't genuinely so) before expressing my humble gratitude for the chance to make myself feel heard and then pulling one or two other stalling tactics out of my butt if need be before wondering something out loud like maybe why couldn't the thought and deed leaders provide a box with a slot built into it so members of the general public like me could hand in a little note that suggested something like having this crop of thought and deed leaders spend a minute at least thinking about why their predecessors didn't think about offering such a suggestion box to earlier generations of the brunt-takers when it comes to the fearless leaders' devastating impacts on civilization way back before it was too late to stop such runaway trains of thought as the one now barreling us all down together on the already mentioned unsunshiny day when the baton of thought and (mis)deed-leading gets passed to the mechanical persuasion of the banes of us earthlings' existence.

Easy, Tiger

1 - Never do I feel better about my share of humanity's god-given dominion over all that god created in the world's very first work week than when I manage to attract the superior gaze of one of our two family indoor housecats of the tom persuasion and use a fabulously communicable slow blinking to trick the disinterested little shit into slow blinking his hilarious way to a state of peaceful respite from the high alert his kind is atavistically always on unless some something like an extra blasé and otherwise chill and unbothered master at slow blinking like me comes along to make it known that the coast is clear enough for a general pride-wide letting of the guard down at least until the fragile peace is broken by the next modern-day imitation of a sound made back in the day when the indoor housecat's ancestors' world was crawling with terrible flesh and blood perils to be on the constant lookout for.

2 - And sure, I do feel a little bad about abusing my dominion over a domesticated onetime creature of the field like one of our family tomcats and cracking up inside about it at that even though I've grossly violated some kind of unspoken social contract by soothing a longstanding member of the household with a sense of security even as his age-old defenses were being sneakily breeched by the same co-head of the household in question telling him with his eyes that all was well enough for him to lower his age-old defenses.

3 - But on the other hand, I'm quite happy with myself for having freed the jumpy little tiger for a while from the clutches of the diehard Darwinian fear that something fitter than him is in the process as per usual of coming along from out of nowhere or maybe everywhere and putting the decided kibosh on his day and also famously night job of doing the very same thing to the similarly hypervigilant things like a poor housefly that he's fitter than.

4 - And speaking of tigers and members of a household and chronic senses of insecurity and violated social contracts and Darwinian overkill and highly communicable ways of behaving, it's too bad there's no way for a highly trained A-level grade rescue team of slow-blinkers to go out there and soothe all the sweet and cuddly little cubs of the tiger moms and the tiger dads madly changing the tiger-stripelessness on the household's little pussycats being outfitted with the keen eye of the tiger for keeping always on any and all openings for reaching the top spot of the food chain and for simultaneously keeping a hypervigilant lookout for the so-called ambush's worth of the other rapacious examples of the tiger-like stripe of onetime pussycat in the constant process of "going and getting 'em" out there in the zero-sum game of life like their go-getting mommy and daddy tigers (as in the sons and daughters of their own mommy and daddy tigers) keep telling their little tigers to go out there and do through word and hugely communicable deed.

5 - It kind of makes a person feel a little bad for the purr- and play-happy pussycats the tiger moms and dads once

were themselves before they let the man and woman-eating tiger enter their proverbial tank for fueling their apex go-getting till they reached dominion over most the descendants of the good lord's proverbial Saturday handiwork when they weren't hypervigilantly busy looking over their shoulder for the so-called streak of slavering and lip-smacking tigers prowling their way toward dominion over them.

6 - It's pretty hard not to see the apex go-getters in question as tigers of the paper variety when you consider what scaredy-cats they are when it comes to letting go of the tiger of rapacious tigerness they've got by the tail madly dragging them along through a stripe-or-be-striped life of do-or-die stripes-earning in a jungle's worth of other apex go-getters of the same stripe of the stripes that never get changed no matter how much closer and closer we keep getting to the day that a worldwide spreading of the super communicable human yawn at long last says it all about the so hopelessly twice-told tale of the tiger-types of human beings reaching all the top spots on the stupid food chain with all their filling of all our shared living spaces with the menacing ever-present sense of perfectly legitimate insecurity keeping us all on this crazy-making high alert making the human equivalents of a truly beautiful thing like a sweet and simple interval of soul-restoring purring and or kittenish playfulness so hard if not impossible to come by.

The Gall

1 - For my money the most fitly christened rule of thumb or truism or homespun canon or principle that humanity has ever come up with is the law a guy named John Gall forever eponymously associated with the common version of the noun "gall" upon introducing the notion to his constantly bit-chomping and gun-jumping brothers and sisters here along this botched double-time march of human progress that slow and steady and incremental ends up winning the race when it comes to stuffing our human systems with all the heaps and gobs and slews of complexity that according to Gall's Law will always dumbly gum up the works of the complex systems in question if these systems haven't been kluged together slowly but surely from a once perfectly working system of the pure and simple persuasion.

2 - Certainly there's not not an argument to be made for the title for one of our woman or man-made natural laws going to Putt's Law as in the one that says that the technological breed of the already mentioned complexity we never stop stuffing into our human systems for some unknown reason is dominated by two types of putzes: the ones who understand what they do not manage and the putzes who manage what they do not understand.

3 - And OK sure, there's also not not an argument for the prize in question going to the law named after a certain early 20th century A-plus student of humanity and author of no less a tome than *The Story of Mankind* who took time out of his busy schedule as a notable Roaring

Twenties and then Depression Era historian to lend his surname of van Loon to the law that says the amount of the mechanical development breed of the already mentioned complexity we stuff into our human systems will always be in inverse ratio to the number of slaves that happen to be at the disposal of the so-called asylum or the cry or the raft or the waterdance of the puffed up and preening loons of a feather who do the deciding about whether it will be slavery of one brand so to speak or another or mechanical development that delivers us all to the next leg of our brutish and so paradoxically also overcomplicated march of human progress into more and more loony brutish overcomplication.

4 - Fine. Some consideration should probably also be extended to the Flynn Effect when you consider that in addition to its namesake (James R. Flynn) the name of the effect in question also calls to mind the Flynn of the swashbuckling Errol variety who lady killingly lent his surname to a longtime popular slang phrase that roughly translates into something like "making a piece of cake out of nailing it with respect to a stab taken at some deed or exploit" like nailing the object of one's hyperactive desire or more broadly like totally screwing everyone under you in a meritocratic setup where according to the Flynn Effect our species keeps swimming in more and more of the disparately divvied IQ points it takes to fill a .civilization with the smarter and smarter smartest guys and gals in the room needed to keep dreaming up new and improved ways for those above to be inner like Flynn than those below when it comes to gaining sanctuary from the Reverse Robin Hood Effect that the Flynn Effect so ironically brings into play.

5 - And no, I haven't forgotten to consider a certain dictum bearing the name of a so-called Lord going by the agonizingly perverse name of Acton in that his indisputable observation that power corrupts and absolute power corrupts absolutely is an obvious call for changing the dumbass top-down social structures that humanity apparently will never "act on".

6 - So anyway, let's all go back to Gall's Law and take notice for a moment of all the gall it takes to fancy yourself qualified to introduce something super smart-sounding like Gall's Law into our human consciousness even though you've obviously not truly scrutinized the societies you're commenting on enough to know better than gallingly to go right along with this ruinous human impulse to keep stuffing heaps and gobs and slews of complexity into all our systems and even more gallingly to concoct an awful pathology-enabling game plan for taking on more and more of this complexity we've been so grossly overmatched by for so long that no matter how much gall and wormwood it keeps blighting our societies with we only grow more ready to let it keep mass producing the sound and the fury we've traded life's simple pleasures in for to our great shame.

Imitation Game

1 - Wouldn't this common ordinary everyday citizen love to chip his share of the wisdom of the masses into the cranking out of the next revised edition of the training manual or rulebook of the proctors or the referees of the Turing Test or the Imitation Game, respectively and respectively in this mad all-out rush to scientifically ascertain whether it's officially time yet for humanity to bask in the glory of our having commemorated the advent of the Anthropocene by ushering in our artificial successors in the turning of everything on Earth to shit.

2 - It would feel so great and be so life-affirming at least for me to impress my common ordinary everyday friends and confound my enemies by having played even some small part in issuing the avouchment for the not unparturitional appearance of the bona fide Adam or Eve figure in the real-life origin story of the *H. machina* race we incidentally can only cross our human fingers and hope will be born a Tuesday's child full of grace maybe or a Sunday's child who is bonny and blithe and good and gay or better yet a Friday's child who is loving and giving as opposed to the mechanical Adam or Eve figure in question being born a Wednesday's child full of woe or god forbid a Saturday's child who's stuck for life like *H. sapiens'* Father figure was with working hard for a living as one of our own origin stories goes.

3 - Of course it would also be great if *H. machina's* Mother or Father figure ended up being born under a kind and

empathetic water sign like Cancer or Pisces and not under a sign like Scorpio, say, or Capricorn.

4 - And ideally it would be before this current year of the peaceful and longevity-blessed Rabbit gave way to another year of the big bad fire-breathing Dragon that we sewed up all this laboring if you will to deliver on our promise to prove beyond doubt that we've literally outsmarted ourselves by artificially blowing the lid off the proverbial box we can't naturally think outside of and thereby letting a next iteration of our so-called human intelligence run even wilder and even freer than the original did on this long seven-deadly-sin-cursed road to this eve of our demonstrating to the most awesome degree so far that for all its vaunted awesomeness our human intelligence in its biological form doesn't give *H. sapiens* the ability to learn anything at all from our lifting the lid on a box of the obvious Pandora's persuasion no matter how many times we keep doing it without learning anything at all if you don't count our learning all the new and improved ways to think about how the fallout from one instance of our idiotic lid-lifting amounts to nothing but a terrific testament to all the progress we're making in our march toward blowing the lid off the next box of the obvious Pandora's persuasion.

5 - Anyway, my notes to the updaters of the training manual or rulebook in question would definitely include the strongly worded suggestion that the proctors or the refs-in-training be super well-groomed for keeping the human ear they're lending to the confabulations between them and the true human being and the algorithm-based faker aping its primate conversation mates wide open for

picking up such dead giveaway clues that a chitchatter is not the proud artificial owner of a truly human intelligence as a less than truly mind-boggling amount of the kinds of intellectual cowardice and dishonesty and the even more mind-boggling paucity of self-awareness it takes to keep using human intelligence stupidly in no small part by using it to a fare-thee-well to super elaborately argue we're not using it stupidly.

6 - I would also train the adjudicators to listen super closely to the back and forth proper and then to the slowed-down recordings of them and then take a high-powered magnifying glass to the transcripts and then to the spaces between the lines of them in search of any signs that the natural thought and speech and tone patterns of a true human interlocutor have been sort of blushily distorted by the unnaturally powerful blast of the sincerest flattery that her or his automated counterpart in the Imitation Game would surely touch off as a special emissary of humanity's so lavish vanity project of second-handedly flattering ourselves by creating greater and greater algorithmic imitators of the most noteworthy trait that separates us from the lower animals if you don't count the incredible collective death wish that makes the lemmings look like raging diehards at the house party of life.

7 - And I would have the arbiters of what's a human train of thought and what's not crank the recordings of the backs and the forths up to 11 if need be to detect whether or not the two Turing Test-takers are emitting the same hint of humanity's signature knocking together of rocks in the head as the flatterer and the flatteree in question

are cudgeling their brains and their circuitry, anti-respectively in their respective attempts to ace their answers to such really good questions as "How would you go about maximizing performance in your own paperclip factory?"

8 - And of course there's got to be some way to train the human eye to spot signs of the spinning head (or, rather, its rough equivalent of the nuts and the bolts and the solder joints variety) that's got to be a by-product of a thinking thing's skyrocketing (or, rather, being skyrocketed) all the way up practically overnight to the king/queen's throne of the Darwinian jungle we *H. sapiens* spent so many eons super strictly following the laws of all the way to the top only then to spawn the probably unstoppable all-leapfrogging pretenders to our own throne of lies as a certain beautiful extra-human truthteller called Buddy the Elf would call it.

Beaching Off with the Barbie Movie

1 - I wish the Barbie movie hadn't made me so sad for humanity as I watched the barbiearchy fail like crazy to be any better at making the world a safer place for one and all than the idiotic patriarchy was for all those generations it apparently spent showing the sisters of the lucky lucky brothers living it up in a meat grinder of their very own over-privileged making everything they needed to know about how to super chauvinistically look down their nose at one big lump of otherness that under

kinder circumstances would easily disaggregate into a bunch of different kinds of fathers and husbands and ex-husbands and sons and boyfriends and brothers and boy cousins and uncles at different points along the continuum of how much our insidious systems of coexistence are making life miserable for the poor souls born into this family of so-called humanity.

2 - Perhaps partisanarchy is a better way to name the social system in a film that hemisects the bejesus out of our poor species with the so predictable effect of ushering in a flooding buttload of the kind of cliquey ickyness that blinds one side of a human divide to the ways they're being worse than the side they're treating like dirt.

3 - The hemisecting in question gets even sillier and more pitiful when you factor in how interchangeable the toxic misandryarchal and manhatriarchal goings on on one side are with all the awful patriarchal nonsense diehardedly taking place on the other side here in the aftermath of its unbelievably dumbass heyday.

4 - It's hard at times to watch the film putting the decided kibosh on the thought of a Great Female Hope Barbie killing the Goliath of humanity's inner dickhead with the kind of kindness that recognizes no dividing line between one of us or one kind of us and another as opposed to what's meaniearchally animating all the toxic Mean Girl Writ Large Barbies and the madly Having it All Barbies and the #KILLALLMEN Barbies and the Karen Barbies and the Tiger Mom Barbies and the Ball Buster

Barbies and the so blindly ambitious Hey Look at Me I'm Killing it While Taking No Shit or Prisoners Barbies.

5 - Even without having Googled her I think I would still have sort of known that Greta Gerwig is a product of an all-girl and then an all-woman private schooling career that seems to have functioned not unlike some kind of Barbie Bubble Sorority House that spares its residents such inconvenient challenges to their worldview and attitude as the truth that the so-called grossly overprivileged boys have now long been routed up one side and down the other of their own schooling or the truth that three out of four of the deaths of despair our more or less equal-opportunity sorryarchy is producing by the tens upon tens of thousands per year and counting are coming at the expense of the men said to have it so much better than the ones said to be pretty exclusively on the wrong side of the power differentials in the already mentioned idiotic patriarchy.

6 - At a particularly awful anomic time like this it's a bit more than a little iffy wisdom-wise if you ask me to filmically make sure the self-absorption-loaded whinyarchy remains the overarching social system of choice on both sides of a sex divide that leaves the brothers and the sisters lobbing hate bombs at the sisters and the brothers, respectively for getting in the way of their respective rising mememearchally to the awesomest spots in the already mentioned sorryarchy barreling us all apocalyptically along toward the logical conclusion of our having so stupidly adopted a de facto motto like...

#KILLALLMENANDALLWOMENEQUALLYALONGWITH
THEPLANETTHEY/WELIVEON.

Eke

1 - I suppose we human beings are owed some feather of feather in our caps for having kept evolving for long enough to be a species that can eke at least this miserable strain of meaning from shit like getting more attention than the next relentless attention getter and belonging to some tribe that's said to be better than the proliferating number of other self-styled better tribes we all keep falling into and accumulating more and more stuff no matter what all the stuff-accumulating does to our poor souls and the place we call home and rising higher and higher above more and more of the beings who used to be like us and vice versa and breaking newer and newer ground in the area of using our human brainpower to keep creeping toward the iteration of the Brave New World that finally spells our doom.

2 - In some ways ours is the opposite story of the amazing dung beetles that chose to stand pat when the whole survival of the fittest regime led them to the big day when all the sloughing off of the species' less than best and brightest delivered the dung beetle family to the doorstep of a future together spent eking sustenance and some insectile species of meaning from dollops of literal shit as opposed to the already mentioned ilks of shit we human beings went on to develop the ability to eke

meaning out of long after the point in our story where the premium on the Darwinian kidney of winning the day against our own brothers and sisters could easily have been tossed out the window.

3 - In other ways, though, our story's not unlike that of the super herculean beetle in question when you compare their amazing ability to roll up to 250 times their weight in shit from some point A to some point B with our human ability to keep shouldering the bigger and bigger loads of the shitty sources of meaning it takes to eke out enough of the precious stuff to keep carrying on in this taking on of more and more shit for lugging from the point A's to the point B's in our march of human progress.

4 - And we're also not un-dung beetle-like in the light so to speak of the nocturnal species of *Scarabaeus* over there in our own Darwinian starting point of the so-called Dark Continent that ingeniously orient themselves using the Milky Way and super scientifically navigate by polarization patterns in moonlight all in the interest of building up the rollable loads of shit for eating meals off of and impressing the opposite sex with and fighting each other for hours at a time over and laying the eggs of the shit-eating babies in so they can later send their own shit-eating babies into the already mentioned future laid out for them by the shit-eating grinners in this Darwinian business of separating the best and brightest shit-kickers if you will from all the rest.

5 - It's too bad, though, that even after all this extra-added evolving on our part we still don't boast the kind of highly refined nose that allows the hunting and gathering dung beetle to know a whiff of shit when it sniffs it in the wind because if we did boast such a nose we'd know in an instant it was bullshit when we told ourselves and each other that it's a big wonderful gusher's worth of Shinola and not nothing but bigger and bigger buttloads of shit we're eking all this measly meaning out of along this road heading in the opposite direction of all the sweeter and less hollow and less shit-like sources of meaning we've permanently turned all our blind noses up at for some dumb unknown reason.

Battle of the Sexes

Here's a handful of one gender-blindish misanthrope's hot takes on this point in the long ongoing Battle of the Sexes where folks like WaPo's Christine Emba and the Brookings Institution's Richard V. Reeves are spearheading our species' lagged response to the pitiful way so many of our boys and men have been acquitting themselves here in these relatively early days of a certain last word in awesome human accomplishment we're fancily calling the Anthropocene as opposed to going with some simpler word or phrase that gets it more clearly across that we've arrived at our last chance to stop doing our cohabitation of this planet all wrong.

1 - One pearl of conventional wisdom going peculiarly undisputed (as per usual) in all this wringing of hands and clutching of pearls over what's become of the boys and the men being undone by the undoing of their male superiority as the story goes is that life was one big bowl of cherries for all echelons of boys and men in the glory days of the patriarchy when one and all with a naturally big or a naturally or an unnaturally enhanced or a little or a micro or a medium-sized male reproductive organ between the legs of our species' trademark bipedalism were free to go out there and lavishly cash in on such unfair shares of personal autonomy as the ones that got all the lower stories of all the working world's notoriously remorseless power structures filled with the stiffs needed for the shit to roll downhill on.

2 - And all the unfair shares of personal autonomy that got all the big manly bodies into the pockets of the black lung and the mesothelioma and all the other brands of bad shit waiting to happen to men called to the mines of the coal and the salt and the asbestos and the uranium and the so-called ladies' best friend variety that have gotten us all so far on this march of human progress toward our already mentioned last chance to stop doing this march of human progress all wrong.

3 - And all the unfair shares of personal autonomy that have supplied the patriarchal husbands and the fathers in both the girl and the boy-featuring families up there at the top of the food chain with all the barely post-adolescent male cannon fodder needed for humanity to keep putting on display one of our most godawful examples of our godawfulness at working out the

differences between us that so paradoxically have done nothing but keep proliferating the harder we males and females of the species and everyone in-between have all worked together in lockstep to make the Anthropocene by far the shortest epoch the world will have ever seen.

4 - And let's not forget the exercises in unfairness that have freed the lucky husbands and the boyfriends and the fathers and the sons up to become big and little and medium-sized fish out of water with regard to the hearth and home they've been liberated from in favor of their duly answering civilization's clarion call for them to get their ass out there and get swimming with the sharks and the would-be sharks in all the big and little and medium-sized ponds where size all along has really really mattered for all involved up to and including the so unlucky ones who've been historically stuck in the confines of the hearth and home while the husbands and fathers and boyfriends and sons have been out there eating the littler fish alive when they haven't been busy being eaten alive by fish that are bigger than them as per the classic capturing of the so oddly still religiously followed laws of the jungle as they apply underwater.

5 - Let's all take a moment right now to recognize a certain tireless humanity-congratulating big fish named Steven Pinker for the part he's played in making it perfectly viable in the context of bemoaning the present-day plight of boys and men for the bemoaners to ignore or gloss over the plight of the boys and men of yore because they (the bemoaners) have felt the need to

spend no energy whatsoever entertaining the possibility that the problem might all along have been the always ongoing awfulness of this dumbass march of human progress that never gets us anywhere near any new systems of coexistence that don't make life miserable for most of the ones shouldering the incumbency on them to go out there and earn their share (and ideally more than their share) of worth (in the eyes, for instance, of the prospective mates mostly uninterested in little fish) often if not almost always by lowering the worth of other fish in comparison to them.

6 - Let's also take a moment or more to acknowledge that one longstanding pearl of conventional wisdom that holds up 100% is the proposition that girls and women have been treated like shit in many many ways when unquestioned patriarchy was the order of the day.

7 - And let's don't even think about questioning the hard and cold and wholly unavoidable reality that boys and men have been prone to letting the social order bring out the worst and most insufferable dickheadedness and assholery in them when they haven't been busy pumping the dickheadedness and assholery in question back into the system in an unvirtuous circle's worth of the worst in humanity for burying the better angels of our nature under.

8 - But also let's don't not refrain from mindlessly taking at face value the premise among the self-impressed male and female hand-wringers and pearl-clutchers in question that it's only a swath of the boys and men who

are blowing it right now with all their flopping around like pitiful little fish out of the working world's already mentioned big and little and medium-sized quantities of pond water where their self-impressed betters are so busy living it up I guess that it can't quite ever occur to them that all the big and little and medium-sized ponds in question are better described as cesspools spilling over with such unbelievably stupid and ruinous ways to relate to one another and Mother Earth and Nature that it's really hard not to wonder how on earth it could be that the so intrepid spearheaders of our lagged response to a swath of our species' boys and men finding themselves between ways to fit into our systems of coexistence could not be struck by the funny feeling that maybe a better lagged response to spearhead is the hugely overdue one to the plain and simple truth that systems of coexistence that do stuff like chew up and spit out whole swaths of humanity are so stupid and ruinous that it's truly stupid and also ruinously inhuman to think it's the duty of the ones being chewed up and spit out to find a way to fit back into the systems their betters are so self-impressedly said to be thriving in there in the luxury of the perches from which they comment on the human progress or lack thereof of the ones failing like they aren't to thrive as the story goes.

9 - Do not get me started on how shittily the self-impressed successful men out there actually acquitting themselves here in the thick of this Anthropocenic shit show they're mostly the ones running for some dumb unknown reason.

10 - As for the up and coming girls and women said to be crushing it as they make such impressive strides in catching up to the self-impressed successful boys and men when they're not ridiculously busy knocking themselves out putting more and more distance between themselves and the boys and men of the lesser variety, how well are they truly doing at this point in human history where you can't buy an open Overton window when it comes to throwing the idea out there that no matter how well-suited newly "empowered" girls and women are for duly milking power for themselves out of our systems of coexistence these systems are no better suited for them than they are for anybody else if it's true (which it isn't) that the hope is for all the members of our race to spend our respective and our collective days on this earth in a better place than one where two out of every three hard-driving girls worldwide are being beaten up mental health-wise as they join the tercile's worth of their thicker-skinned sisters in growing too good for the boy and menfolk who don't share their wherewithal for hard-drivingly killing it out there in the getting ahead of the next gal or the next guy or the latest disgracefully less than best version of one's own self?

11 - Or a world where the unluckiest members of our race are said to be the ones who can't put enough hard-bought distance between themselves and the latest Oprahesque less than best version of themselves because they're unfairly stuck half the time in the hearth and home with the bumbling and pudgy little balls and chains also known as the human girl and boy babies that so incorrigibly open up the faucets and sometimes even the floodgates on a certain love hormone known to poison even the most fevered dreams of achieving higher and

higher achieving as one great way to give super aggressive vent to the astounding amounts of animus that build up in a gender when the unfair sex spends no end of generations ostentatiously spending all their already mentioned unfair shares of the personal autonomy it takes to be the ones who get to go out there and fight tooth and nail with their fellow human beings for the glorious honor of making the history before it's too late because all the history and all the herstory-making is barreling us nothing but closer and closer to the perfectly foreseeable moment when human history and human herstory are beside the point because none of us are left anymore to keep repeating the stupid apocalyptic shit we kept doing to ourselves and one another whether we learned the victors' and or the losers' versions of history and herstory or not.

12 - And speaking of astounding amounts of animus, to the really mean girls writ large out there responsible for making shit like hashtag KILLALLMEN an actual thing in the human history and human herstory barreling us all together toward their own sad last chapters, congratulations on soaking up so much of the chauvinistic dickheadedness and assholery that as mentioned have been pumped into the systems of your protested coexistence with the boys and men you've opened season on with your hard-boiled outpouring of so much animus of the Jungian variety and otherwise that you're drawing closer and closer and ever closer by the day to pulling off the unheard of herstory-making miracle of outperforming even the dipshits and shitheads in the dumbass manosphere in subjecting everybody to the toxic tough guy routines that have become so indispensable to the Karens of our species and

to the tiger moms and to all the unapologetic ball-busters and even to all the righteous callers on the awful boys and men to adopt the anima traits that nobody in this so-called civilization respects anymore not even the ones calling on the awful boys and men to tap super kindly and gently and tearfully into them.

13 - Speaking of the so-called anima traits, and going back to the sweet and innocent and also objectively adorable and really neat-smelling (especially around the wispy-haired head area when they're sweating a little in their unbelievably sweet sleep) little girl and boy babies, what in the world did all the ever-growing population of single moms and their much much rarer fatherly counterparts and all the kicked-out and all the absconding and all the workaholic and all the other kinds of tangential dads and all the coequal and the egregiously singular wearers of the pants in the two-parent households of the one and the two and the brutally no breadwinner variety alike think was going to happen in this stupid human experiment when everyone and their dumb mother and their dumb father (and their possibly even dumber step mother and step father) decided in unusual unison that they weren't botching the shit out of their most important jobs at all in tanking the chances of the species' sweet little babies to go on to lead decent and meaningful lives that go undarkened by shit like the awful epidemics of mental health problems you get when you get your systems of coexistence all wrong without ever doing your job of correcting them if not for your disgracefully self-interested self and or for your own human brothers and sisters at least for the ones human existence has put you in charge of protecting?

14 - Decent and meaningful lives, by the way, that also don't end in the terrible deaths of despair that come in such heart-breaking clusters of three boys for every girl when our boy and girl babies' own moms and dads keep abysmally failing to take to the streets in protest of their own abysmal failure to work together in child-proofing the world so their own sweet and innocent and formerly adorable and really neat-smelling little girls and boys writ large don't end up going out there like they themselves did thanks to their own so low-performing moms and dads and playing (for keeps) all day long with all the sharp and all the pointy and all the red-hot and all the electrical and otherwise crazy dangerous shit that accessorizes the runaway tribal and highly individualized narcissistic and materialistic way of life that keeps making the more and more dangerous world so much safer and safer for the toxic self-interestedness that even a dumbass bunch like us has come to realize in our hearts and our guts and by way of our best and brightest self-interested agenda-free studiers of us ourselves is nothing but the dead end we nonetheless will apparently never stop barreling toward together from all our respective super special and hyper-individualistical and also tribal and extra-sacred personal identity-shaping locations at the dead center of the universe.

Grand Achievement

1 - It's a bit ridiculous the steep premium we human beings keep putting on the grand achievements that in world record time have fetched us all up to this Anthropocene being so predictably governed by the ones with the strongest weakness for reaching higher places than everybody else and by the Promethean geniuses who keep making the breakthroughs into the Braver New Worlds where the so-called game-changers reign somehow without ever really changing this game of Life being won all the time by the ones who scratch and claw their way over the others on their way up to the top and the ones blazing trails into the same old over-charted territory where the grand achievers get to write their own first-class tickets when they're not busy also writing the second and the third and worse-class tickets of the low-achievers being run into the ground by all these amazing breakers of the new ground that when it comes down to it is nothing really but the same old earth that's already been broken a thousand or more times over by the hundreds upon hundreds of generations' worth of the incredible fetchers of us all up to this juncture in the march of human progress where it's hard not to wonder what manner of planetary epoch comes after the one we ourselves of course have called the already mentioned Anthropocene.

2 - You'd think we self-styled *H. sapiens* would long ago have started rethinking the grossly oversized premium we put on the overachieving that separates the sheep from the goats acronymically associated with the sorts of feats and deeds and exploits and master strokes that

leave the sheep tediously bleating all the oohs and ahs and all the hosannas when they're not busy muttonheadedly flocking to the next field of opportunity to be fleeced by these Greatest Overachievers of All Time who keep outdoing the GOATs before them in this already mentioned fetching of us all up to the planetary epoch preceding the one there'll be none of us super special dubbers of stuff left around to slap a fancy Latin-based name on.

3 - Given all the power there's said to be in numbers you'd think the steep premium would be placed on a sheepish genus of medium or low-achievement or some respectable something in-between as opposed to the higher and higher achievement of our species' best and brightest power-grabbing GOATs who after all are outnumbered by a mile by the woolgathering kinds of fluffy ruminant if you will who nice and easily achieve the feat of looking just like one of the fluffy clouds they have their muttonheads in while with equal ease they polish off the feat of symbolizing gentle affection and peaceful coexistence and manage with a little help from a relatively mild-mannered bellwether to go mostly with the flow occasioned by the subtle forces in charge of the sheep community's undertaking of a plain and simple group project like the flocking that comes so easily to a species whose name is beautifully both singular and plural all at the same time.

4 - And the above is to say nothing of a sheep flock's natural talent for making the odd peace-breaking blackguard in the community really self-consciously stand out and nor is it to mention the help the super

friendly and surprisingly nimble meadow fence-hopping sheep quite readily lined up at all times to other-centeredly extend to the members of our human community having no end of trouble getting the much needed sleep that gets harder and harder to come by in this world as fouled up as Hogan's goat so to speak thanks to the gross overachievers the sheep have ceded their power in numbers to for some unknown muttonheaded reason.

5 - But upon further rumination if you will perhaps we low-to-medium-achieving muttonheads have actually gotten it right by placing a sky-high premium on grand achievement and the one and only problem (and perhaps a solvable one at that) is that what we've been calling achievements of the grand variety are actually the exact opposite of grand and could be easily seen as such were they ever set up next to a mind-blowing human achievement like getting all the overachievers under control so we could maybe all flock along together into greener pastures where gentle affection and peaceful coexistence are the order of the livelong day.

The Bottom of it All

1 - From my armchair here on the sidelines it's getting odder and odder to watch the cosmologically and the ontologically-minded queriers of the proliferating weirdnesses way down there and way up and out there in the quantum world and its astronomical counterpart, respectively as they train their amazing compliments of brainpower on everything it seems but the huge repeating news flash that the universe has been leading the science types on a never-ending merry chase since the day in that imaginary territory commonly known as the past when the mythical founding mother or father of the science types in question first stuck her or his perhaps still large, broad nose (as the Darwin story goes) in the universe's business of growing only more mysterious the more we poke our more and more refined noses in its business.

2 - From my Monday morning quarterback's point of view it seems outlandishly obvious that the universe is never going to cough up whatever one missing thing it would take for our jury-rigged conception of how the universe works to smack of anything less slapped together than this kluge that only loses more units of its dwindling legitimacy with each new moving part that has to be added to it thanks to some new breakthrough into new unbelievably fertile ground when it comes to springing up the next set of breakthroughs that need to be made to get to the next set of breakthroughs that need to be made and so on as our bodged-together conception of it all wantonly violates no end of physical laws by

never collapsing, as one example, under the greater and greater weight of its nature as an unnatural lash-up.

3 - With all the efficaciousness of yelling at the game on the television I have yelled like a madman at the books churned out by the science types who refuse to deduce that the universe has mousetrapped them into making it all up for us as we go along on this all-out snipe hunt of a looking high and low for the slippery thingamajig or thingamabob or whatchamacallit needed for the Rube Goldbergian edifice of our sense of how this existence is built to make sense instead of threatening all the time to come tumbling down around all the science types in the middle of their mad turning of the world inside out and upside down in their looking high and low for the wild goose of a final answer to the question "What in the world is the universe up to?"

4 - Perhaps most irking to this admitted goober over here in the peanut gallery is the mulish refusal of so many of the science types to believe their own eyes when they see that there's no such thing as the raw materials they're using to produce such impossibly convoluted avatars of our current thinking about what the universe is up to as a certain living document called the Standard Model.

5 - Whether they want to admit it to themselves or us or not, they themselves have taken us to a place (or the illusion thereof) where it's not really honest or possible to think that divisibility is really a thing.

6 - No matter how snugly they've ensconced themselves together there in the safety of a so-called base unit going by the name of the Planck length there's no way multiplicity is really a feature of this setup where everything in every area of scientific inquiry only makes some modicum of sense if you don't keep drilling down till you get to the point where either you admit there's no such thing as a standalone thing like a point or you invoke some timeworn forces like the crazy vagaries of knowability to hold onto your determination to keep forging ahead in all this forging of overgrown bodies of knowledge with raw materials that are nothing but a runaway overmuch of nothing.

7 - Two and a half thousand or so of these falsehoods called years ago a fiction called Parmenides at least knew better than to take up the fool's errand of putting the semblance of distance between himself and the fact of the matter so to speak that the only thing inhabiting the elbow room that each putative unit of matter must have by definition is the elephant of roomlessness the science types must keep turning a blind eye to if discontinuity is to continue being a centerpiece of the common wisdom about how to sort everything out in a universe determined to make the science types strain every nerve to keep cleaving and hewing to the point of view that it's all been cleaved and hewed into a near infinity of things longer than a Planck length with nothing under the sun to fill up the "space" between things if you don't count the cloud of figurative crickets you can practically hear all over again out there every time a question is asked about what manner of filler it is that makes it possible to think of the cosmos as the home of untold tons upon tons of

singletons instead of just one all-inclusive one that doesn't weigh a single thing.

8 - Since Zeno, the science types have really been getting nowhere in the distancing of themselves from the game-changing revelation that an arrow can't very well get from a point A to a point B when there's no end of intermediary points between them and no end of intermediary points between the intermediary points and this is not even to mention that there's no such thing as any of the points in question and it's also not even to mention that the arrow itself melts into oneness with every other thing that isn't really a discrete thing without help from all the holders of the line when it comes to drawing no end of lines between and around purely illusory units of the fundamental stuff that the illusions of bigger stuff are made of.

9 - And how in the world do these holders of the line explain the tippy tippy tippy (times near infinity) tip of the arrow in question almost no sooner entering the foggy swamp of its trajectory's first Planck length that's not supposed to be crossable in the traditional sense than it impossibly exits the swamp in question on its way into and then out of the next uncrossable foggy swamp of a Planck length and so on in a phenomenal string of crossings that lead straight as an arrow if you will to the good point that if the Planck length can be crossed in the traditional sense after all then the same tradition kind of insists that some fraction of the full crossing must have happened and called into question the nonsense that the nonsensical Planck length is as small a thing as there is?

10 - And are these impossibly long strings of Planck lengths supposed to be butting up against one another, and if they are how do you tell them apart and how is it that they don't make up one thing way bigger than its individual constituents and what's to keep one of these so-called smallest things in the universe from bleeding a tiny bit into another and or vice versa and thereby sort of Venn diagrammatically producing a thing smaller than either of the two Planck lengths that mothered and fathered it, and if these long strings of Planck lengths aren't butting up against each other what is it that's between them (crickets again) and is whatever it is smaller than the Planck lengths it's meant tidily to divide into foggy units of the tiniest thing possible thanks to the science type who came up with a constant that also bears the Planck name?

11 - As much as divisibility can't really be a real thing, the mythical infinite version of it does help us put on the figurative table (if that's not too dumb a redundancy in this rant against the notion of physicality) the big problem with the popular position if you will that the universe is quantumly bristling with little jots and dots and iotas and a growing number of other sorts of whatnots that with many many varying degrees of fleetingness take up positions in spacetime when they're not busy zipping from one of these positions to another at rates that are said to be perfectly ascertainable as long as the science types don't try to ascertain them at the same time (whatever that means) that they're nailing down the position of the little zipper from the position in question.

12 - The problem is this: how on earth can an ostensible thing be said to hold a spatial position at any given so-called point in time when the number of coordinates for designating a location in an infinitely divisible whatsit like spacetime is unlimited, and this is not even to get into the issue of relativity?

13 - Doesn't this rabbit hole of unlimitedness mean that there's not really any spatial or temporal place for things to be even if there were such a thing as things?

14 - Isn't the physicalist position scissored into oblivion by all the runaway divisibility that goes on below the false bottom of the Planck length when we stop pretending that the length in question settles all the paradoxes besetting our concept of a thing getting from one place a thing can be said to be to another?

15 - What, precisely, are the points in spacetime where/when the collapsing wave functions in every numberless hole and corner of this world in this universe all give rise to another one of those innumerable knock-offs of the world in question that many science types posit seemingly out of a reflexive need to keep foisting multiplicity on our notions of what it is the scrutinizers of our universe are working with?

16 - When the collapsing wave functions in question make their respective plays for having taken place at some specific point in spacetime, at what specific point does the universe decide that all the dropping like a rock

in the bottomless sea of possible coordinates has gone on long enough for the ubietyless collapses in question to instantaneously (whatever that's supposed to mean) give rise to those other worlds out there also apparently crawling with diehard science types refusing to deduce that the universe is made up of some other stuff than the stuff and nonsense piling up in this kluging together of a narrative starring various illusory schools of red herrings sending us in every which direction in this sea of ubietylessness but the one that gets us to the eureka moment when as one if you will the science types finally see there really truly honestly is no such thing as a moment or anything other than a oneness so singular as to altogether dissolve a certain key tool in all this mass producing of fabrications called mathematics.

17 - It's not un-heartening that a lot of the science types and their philosopher analogs have returned once again to admitting that all this scientific beating of the universe's bushes for the deep secrets the universe seems to keep keeping from them has turned up nothing more high-priority than the hard consciousness problem.

18 - It likewise seems kind of promising that some of the ones undertaking to ravel (as in unravel as opposed to the opposite thing that ravel can mean in our duality-centric way of thinking and talking about things) the big tangled problem in question are not holding for dear life (whatever that is) onto the mind-body dualism that comes with the territory when a putter of consciousness under the microscope is oriented toward discontinuing the notion that discontinuity isn't a thing.

19 - It's great that the grind of science has micronized the grinders enough for their sister and brotherhood to include the kinds of bold goers into the unknown who place consciousness at the center (wherever that is) of reality by way of such bodies of thought (minus the body) as Panpsychism and Emergentism and Neutral Monism and all kinds of Idealism and Conscious Realism and Biocentrism and Relational Quantum Mechanics and so on.

20 - What's a lot less great, though, is that these bodies of thought keep keeping one foot far too solidly (if "solidly" is a word that can be attached to a figment like a foot with no place anywhere but another figment to plant itself) in the physicalists' camp while the other foot is working urgently for purchase in a consciousness-based cosmology made unavoidable by the ongoing miserable failure of the universe's material stuff to hold up under all the figurative and all the literal microscopes it's been put under by so many science and philosophy types having a hard problem with believing their own eyes when they keep telling them there's no there or when there for playing home to a bunch of material stuff.

21 - Why on earth are the bold throwers of time and space and spacetime out the window like the Biocentrists, say, or the Conscious Realists, so prone to invoking space- and time- and spacetime-dependent fictions like biology and Darwinism in making the case that reality dissolves into consciousness or something

like it when time and space and spacetime are thrown out the window?

22 - Why not just get the going of the whole spurious nine yards over with for goodness sake?

23 - Instead of doing stuff like stuff a fabrication like the human brain into the equation so it can satisfy the knee-jerk dualist need for a thing other than consciousness all by itself to be the origin of consciousness, I wish the science and philosophy-types out there at the leading edge of our getaway from physicalism would listen better to the amazing illusion of human brains telling them that they must be nothing but the playthings of a broader all-involving consciousness that has mousetrapped them and the rest of us into conjuring up an impossibly complicated and always more elaborate-growing shaggy dog story for covering over our roles as the immaterial playthings of a timeless and spaceless and objectless consciousness of an all-involving nature.

Footnote

Of course all the above could simply be a matter of my having been mousetrapped myself into adding all the above to the process of kluging an illusory conception of the universe together. (The thought admittedly gives me a bit of a solipsistic thrill.)

It could also, of course, be that we anti-physicalists have been duped into our positions by a human brain-centered consciousness that evolutionarily grew cruel or fun-loving enough to produce the mere illusion that reality is a mere illusion.

But also maybe the illusion that reality is an illusion is the mere illusion. And who knows how many other such possibilities are out there waiting to be created out of thin consciousness if that really is all there is to reality and out of whatever else if it isn't?

All I can say is that my poor grossly over-cudgeled brain right now really wouldn't mind a timeless and spaceless spell of the famous peace of mind that so many science and non-science-types alike have arrived at by way of their magic mushroom-driven trips and their near-death experiences and their full and their half and their quarter (and so on I suppose) lotus positions.

Cave Man

1 - It's hard to imagine a state nickname attached more aptly to one of our species' American senatorial wonder boys than The Cave State is to the so-called Honorable Josh Hawley even though there's no way "honorable" is how any honorable constituent of his in The Show-Me State would ever describe this bad example of humanity in general and manhood in specific (using any definitions there are) that the famously fist-pumping scurrier to personal safety from the numbnutses worked up by incendiary rhetoric and fist-pumping like his has shown himself to be over and over again even as he's cos-playingly taking it upon himself (at the super courageous risk of being too on the nose in his manly-man role-

playing) to super duper aggressively champion the cause of the Cave Men he basically says America and the world need the alpha sex to be all over again if we don't want the ladies and the brainiacs and the elitist pinkos and all the nancies and the epicureanistas apparently even effeter than all the rest of them put together to turn the Lord's own chosen master sex into a worldwide slumber party's worth of girly men who think they've got better things to do than bare-chestedly show the world who's boss because of all the right macho stuff their Y chromosomes are naturally made out of.

2 - The senator from The Lead State (just saying) has gotten it in his super fastidiously groomed head that it's he-mandatory if you will for the human brotherhood of men and boyfolk to put all their yang and animus traits on display all the time for its own sake as opposed, say, to keeping their manly cave-manliness on hold but always poised for busting out in such moments calling for red-bloodedly dropping the club or the hammer as the crossing of paths with the fraudulent likes of a Josh Hawley or a bow-tied Richie Rich Boy like Tucker Carlson asking if not begging for a good bitch-slapping for mansplaining to grown-ass men how to go about conducting themselves in this all-out Losing Battle of the Sexes (where the distaff side in droves, by the way, is super duper empoweredly joining the side they can't beat unless you count the beating of the staff side in question at its own game of lopsidedly making the yang and animus traits the ones that make the so stupidly doomed world go 'round).

3 - Going back for a moment to the famously ruffle-shirted and twinkle-toed and otherwise certainly metrosexuality-curious Richie Rich Boy and strongman fanboy and alleged tough guy in his own right going pretty predictably by the prep-schoolboyish name of Tucker Carlson (he went to prep school in the yacht capital of the world after all) it would be awesome if some somehow more enlightened version of the kind of larger than life authoritarian Father Figure like Viktor or Vladimir or Recep or Jair that the tough guys of the free world are so free to be hopelessly boy-crazy over would put a firm but very caring right hand down there on Tucker's left shoulder and urged him to take time out from his super busy schedule of making the already mentioned Senator Josh Hawley almost look like an honorable man in comparison to him so Tucker would be free for a mike or two as they say in a super butch outfit like the military to really squeeze his eyes closed and clench his little man-fists and his whitened little man-teeth (and perhaps his similarly whitened asshole) and pinch his wry-smile-happy lips together and double down on the signature furrowing of his manly manscaped brow in the not un-tantrum-like effort of doing his very manly utmost to summon enough of the already mentioned right stuff from all his Y chromosomes to find the man-defining courage and emotional toughness and zest for risk-taking and for competing against the next guy (tough or otherwise) it would take for him to subdue the little self-pissing chickenshit in him getting in the way of his looking at himself in the daily make-up-room mirror not as an opportunity again to see how pleased he is with his well rouged and self-certain self (and of course with his face's famous ability on command to fraudulently rise to that Pecksniffian level of moral horror over anything a lefty

says) but as a moment of truth for choosing whether or not to watch himself choose between being a mouse or being a man man enough to admit he's being a little dickheaded mouse with all his sissy-shaming of the so-called mama's boys and the dreaded epicenes and the veritable hen party's worth of chickenhearted capons adulterating the ranks of the master sex being neutered right and left if you believe what Tucker says while he himself is busy making it clear as can be that he's never had anything close to the so-called balls or the classic manly honor to do something with his overprivileged life that doesn't involve a chickenshitted cashing in on a society-toxifying dishonesty of the intellectual and every other variety.

4 - As for that other elitist blamer of the elite for emasculating the master sex (making it really hard to tan their junk or deliver a good tea-bagging and rendering some attachments on the electric manscaper terribly unnecessary among other stuff), it would be awesome if thanks to some healthy amount of ayahuasca or some other closed mind altering substance some big, strong extra father-figure-like alpha Neanderthal in Josh's distant paternal line took him aside and with furrowed beetle-brow (and perhaps the rheumy evolutionary precursor of a not unwomanly dewiness in the unusually huge brown eyes) told Josh he was really worried about him over how much and how aggressively he seemed to be overcompensating for what seemed to be an utter lack of the honorable variety of the yang and animus traits he and the other faces of the first-wave male re-empowerment movement were maybe cheerleading so loudly and repetitiously and so up-and-down-jumpingly and otherwise annoyingly for that they were turning

their intended audience off to the turning off of their yin and anima side even while the punchable faces in question were making it easier and easier for the already mentioned up and coming ladies to channel the hell out of the side of themselves that has no problem at all with the thought of bitch-slapping the self-satisfaction out of a couple of human douchebags like Josh Hawley and Tucker Carlson.

5 - Speaking of whom, you could do worse than choose these two peaches as the Exhibits A and B in the case against a race that at this late date in its reputed evolution is still making nothing but more and more room for the cream of our worldwide crop of utter flops to keep man-spreading themselves so thickly all over the popular imagination as to altogether gum up the works of our using the wonders of evolutionary improvement to make something better out of ourselves than this race of promise-squandering yahoos with the apparently unbreakable habit of spitting out one ugly stunted wonder boy (or girl now) after another for making you wonder what on earth is wrong with us all.

Things Bad Begun

1 - While tomorrow and tomorrow and tomorrow is super busy creeping day to day to the last syllable of recorded time at this pace growing less and less petty by the day if not the minute, it's hard not to think of a certain cursed play of the Scottish persuasion starring the she and he team of climb-aholic balls of fire going by a family name that means "Son of Life" as if this early 17th-century rendering of this 11th-century precursor of the modern-day power couple embodied something fundamental in all of us poor players strutting and fretting our respective hours upon the stage of this similarly cursed tale of our overall human existence being told by the idiot filling it with a lot of nothing-signifying sound and fury till all our yesterdays are done lighting us fools to the tomorrow after which we're mercifully heard no more.

2 - It makes you wonder which long bygone yesterday it was when the Son of Life being played in the cursed idiot-told tale in question by all of humanity all together as one was/were in bad blood and also the regular kind of blood stepped in so far that should he/we have waded no more returning would have been as tedious as to go o'er to the now not so far shore where the brief candle making the walking shadow out of this one big hopelessly show-stealing Son of Life goes out out of some kind of age-old and worldwide spite toward the boneheaded sorts of life-owners who deserve to be heard no more.

3 - Even a stone-blindly ambitious product of the Dark Ages like Macbeth could see the jig was up when Birnam

Wood picked up and took its show on the road and here we inheritors of the breakneck go-getting that did the Macbeths in still can't get enough of all the go-getting here in the thundering middle of this stampede of hardwood trees heading west like there's no tomorrow and tomorrow and tomorrow and this shocking yomp's worth of softwood trees heading north and up the mountainsides at a hardly petty pace toward the point where they've got nowhere left to go to escape the climatic ramifications of humanity's setting of the world on fire as we fireballs of the suicidally self-satisfied variety like to call it.

4 - And even a terrible vessel of medieval sensibilities like Lady Macbeth (who after all was by her own account capable of something like plucking her motherly nipple from the gums of her smiling baby Macbeth and dashing the brains of the little over-reacher-in-training out in the name of go-getting) at least could feel an unappeasable squeam when the still small voice within kept never letting her forget about the blood famously spotting her over-grasping hands and her Lord and Liege at least felt enough stabs of conscience to famously lose sleep over the over-grasping hand he had in a volume of bloodletting overtopped literally millions upon millions of times over by all these more modern-day successors of the Macbeths with the Teflon hands and the skin too thick for a stab of conscience to reach them at all much less cost them any sleep after another long hard power-grabbing day spent thickening the sick plot of this tale being told by the already mentioned idiot.

5 - It all makes you wonder what longer and longer-ago yesterday it was when power hunger joined the regular kind of hunger in madly driving the forerunners of the

Son of Life family along all the tomorrows and tomorrows and tomorrows that led our sorry race to the yesterday when the Bard took quill in hand and forever memorialized the great woefully ignored point that "Things bad begun make strong themselves by ill."

Actualizing Actually

1 - It really wears a poor aging fella out being Jungianly roped into all this stupid misusing of the collective entelechy that's barreling us all a mile or more a minute toward the full and complete realizing of our potential for hopelessly blowing our potential as a collection of organisms invested since day one like all the other organisms are with the power to perfect our given nature instead of letting this whole go-for-broke thing when it comes to going after a goal make us miss some turn we should have taken into a beautiful green field of opportunity to slow ourselves down enough to be caught up with by the sneaking suspicion and or the funny feeling that maybe goal-chasing for its own crazy-making rapacious sake isn't the best use of an inherent life force with the juice to put us in tune with our truer nature by helping us set our sights on fulfilling a fulfillment-loaded goal like slowing ourselves down enough to smell the roses so beautifully showing us how to go about congruently being the things we are.

2 - On cold days I can really feel it in the psychic equivalents of the old joints that have had such a toll

taken on them by all the goes at going against a raging social flow that itself is a matter of going against a flow that would gently take the human organism to a much better place than one where instead of resting on the plentiful laurels earned by getting such wonderful stuff done together as learning to walk upright so we could see more of the beauty exuded by the other organisms entelechially going about the business of doing their thing out there (and such other wonderful stuff as coming up with the words for doing our best to express stuff like wonder) we throw ourselves into never not aspiring to the life of mindless goal-chasing prescribed in these times by the Oprahs and the Joels and the likewise handsomely remunerated profusion of other self-improvement gurus of the world who do so much damage to the human potential for feeling a thing called being happily satisfied with who we are with all their nonstop cues to never let ourselves become un-unsatisfied enough with ourselves that we don't fall all over each other paying dearly for the ticket to hop onto such next bandwagons as the prosperity gospel and the growth mindset and now a new and improved self-improvement movement called manifestation that empowers acolytes to use the currency of nothing but wishful and envy-driven thought to go shopping in the superstore of the whole cosmos for the shiny stuff it takes to become versions of themselves who are better than the ones letting others get ahead of them in gobbling and snapping up the shiny stuff that makes some of us better versions of ourselves than others are of themselves.

3 - Here even half a world away I can feel in my poor bones the reverberating hits the autonomous psyche

takes thanks to the better and better versions of goal-chasing being reached over there in The Land of the Rising Sun where a bunch of our fellow human organisms have changed the age-old nature of the Sun itself with their effectively never letting it set on all the proverbial hay-making of those poor souls who've become versions of themselves who are forced to coin such horrible words as the one meaning "death from work" (*karoshi*) and such sad axioms as the one registering an utter resignation to such states of affairs as the one forcing them to add a word like *karoshi* to their working vocabulary if you will and such states of affairs as the one making a mockery of their beautiful word for the joyous order of pursuit that gets a human organism buoyantly up in the morning (*ikigai*) and such states of affairs as the one leaving them resigned to hopelessly going along with a sad axiom registering an utter resignation to dumb and unnatural states of affairs (*shikata ga nai*).

4 - I wonder if the day will ever come when our dumb organism starts entelechially setting goals more worthy of who we could be like aspiring in Esperanto maybe (while taking full advantage perhaps of the German knack for packing a sentence into a word and the Scandinavian knowhow when it comes to softly crushing it with a word like "lagom") to coin a magic new universal word for living by that refers to the whole-body glow that comes with setting goals according to a happy understanding that slow and steady actually obviates all the racing to see which human organisms can best use a beautiful thing like the already mentioned bipedalism to show everybody that they're made of more special stuff

than their own sisters and brothers of the same special and also the same special persuasion.

Poof!

1 - My own aging but still amazing (as the story goes) three pounds' worth of human brain's got me wondering these days if there's maybe some degree of equivalency between what was going on between the ears and under the dumb powdered wigs of Versailles' highborns back in the turbulent earlyish Enlightenment times and what's taking place in the ostentatious gray matter of the present day thought leaders the Age of Reason vaulted into the ivory towers rising so Bastille-like high above all the intellectual peasants getting restless as natives with all the new and improved iterations of the seigneurial feudalism that left it to the serfs to do all the dirty work that keeps accumulating like nobody's business when a so-called Smart Set that doesn't have to do the dirty work in question is calling all the shots when it's not busy calling all the tunes the serfs and the new versions of the serfs in question are left to dearly pay the piper for.

2 - I also wonder if in the literally rolling heads of the seigneurs of yore there didn't evanescently pop the thought that they maybe might have been half a skosh or so better at the old noblesse oblige or maybe as their grossly overprivileged lives were flashing before their eyes they even almost a little redeemingly wished they still had a fabulously manicured and well be-baubled and

baby-soft hand available for covering their lead-based painted face as a short-lived blush of embarrassing shame came pouring through all the already mentioned lead-based paint about to be outdone whiteness-wise by the next-level blanch that comes with the louisette-delivered death that perhaps couldn't come soon enough for these beau and haut monders mortified (one likes to think) by the virtual sight of a whole life occupied by such ridiculously silly shit as waiting impatiently for the ladies in waiting to help gather up all the metal and the wires and the feathers and cork and horsehair and gauze and cloth and pomatum and clay curlers and bijouterie and other sorts of gewgaws and a stuffed exotic bird or two and a cornucopia of fruit and vegetables and other materials for organizing a still life and the silk ribbons and little pillows and the powders and maybe even an 18th century kitchen sink and things one might find up the ass of a Christmas goose all so one of the court's stupid hairdo engineers could construct such sky-high monuments to the stupidity of pyramidal social structures as the *pouf au sentiment* or the *pouf a la circumstance* designed for commemorating some *beau monde* event every bit as dumb as the commemorating of it in a lady's two or three-foot pyramidal *pouf a la circumstance.*

3 - And the above is to say nothing of such mortifying sights madly flashing before the poor eyes as the cumulative swarm of daily-applied beauty marks named after a shit-eater like the *mouche* or sights like the goofy featherheaded moves in courtly courtship dances like the *canarie* and the also not un-albatrossian *sarabande* or of course sights like all the breeding of the in- variety and all the highly refined and otherwise specialized

tight-laced body language for wearing one's rarefied view of the peasantry on a ruffly sleeve and any number of other ways in the French Revolutionary days for the beau and haut monders to practically beg for a date with The National Razor.

4 - And now every ounce of my personal three pounds' worth of amazing *H. sapiens* brain is making me really wonder if the just-mentioned two or three-foot-high *poufs* aren't a little bit equivalent to the so noticeable aura of gaudy self-importance glowing over the already swelled head area of such Ivory Tower dwellers as a thought-leading brightsider even among the thought-leading brightsiders like the Harvardian Steven Pinker who spends book after lucrative book and talk after self-spotlighting talk safeguarding his cushy spot where the thought leaders are said to belong by protesting too much that all is going super swimmingly here in the already mentioned pyramid he's way way up there near the golden ben ben stone of (along, famously, with the likes of the Jeffrey Epsteins and the also Harvardian Alan Dershowitzes of the world) and arguing that even the intellectual peasants way down there at the pyramid's base should know better than to question their betters when they keep telling them with the straightest of faces and also over and over again and again that everything's going great for them and theirs and will just keep going greater and greater and besides even if things weren't and aren't and won't be going so great they've still always got in their pocket (so to speak) all the thought leaders needed to solve the more and more awful problems the self-serving thought leaders will never stop getting us all into until the natives finally get restless enough to keep shivering this idiotic pyramid until the big tall stupid

pointy thing collapses in its own footprint for good with a big poof! if you will or of course until all the thought-leading leads us unthinkably to the stupid logical conclusion of our letting a preposterously unresponsive Smart Set keep calling all the already mentioned shots and tunes for us all.

5 - Going all the way back for a moment to the already mentioned so-called break from the Dark Ages called the Age of Reason, it seems hardly unreasonable here several blood-stained and otherwise embarrassing centuries later to ask the know-it-alls most prodigally wielding the vaunted powers of reason why with their superior compliment of reason they think it is that the powers in question aren't even strong enough to activate an overhead lightbulb representing an enlightened state where it's plain as day that not only are the vaunted powers of reason unequal to the simple task of teasing out the patent array of reason's treacherous failings but they're also no match for the gut and the funny and the bad and the creepy feelings and the feelings in the bones and in a person's water as they say and the vague ideas and the sneaking suspicions and the sixth sense telling the madly anti-intellectualizing masses that the reason-wielding Enlightenment types have been up to nothing all along but the making of the Dark Ages look like child's play when it comes to ruinously misusing the gifts the endlessly mysterious universe has equipped us with and when it comes to shitting profusely on a beautiful thing like the *anima mundi.*

Banality Galore

1 - It is the afternoon of June 14, 1934 and a human tool going by the name of Adolf Hitler is in the so-called City of Masks having his picture taken as he uses his probably smallish right Heil-Hitlering hand to shake the right hand of a quite likely big and thick-mitted human tool going by the name of Benito Mussolini so that 89 years and two months and 23 days later yours truly could stumble online upon this immortalized moment in our glorious human history when one of our species' paparazzi of the fittingly Italian persuasion snapped a shot of this utter glut of food for thought about what it means to be one of us stupid human beings.

2 - For some context, it is the same date in human history that in a packed latter-day Roman gladiator arena in the so-called Empire City a German fella going by the super manly name of Max Baer brutally proves (Google it if you don't believe me) to the world to be the world's very best beater up of other human beings by beating the ever-loving human shit out of a huge former world's best beater up of other human beings going suitably by the name of Primo Carnera when you consider that super interestingly he was an Italian fella just like the big and thick-mitted human tool we last saw shaking hands happily with the little-mitted Teutonic human tool even though the former would go on super astutely to dub the latter "a silly little monkey".

3 - For a little more human historical context before we tuck into the already mentioned food for thought, an

even dozen years to the day after the glorious moment in human paparazzo history in question a certain paternally pure German and huge but smallish-handed apprentice-firing human tool and world-class nicknamer self-nicknamed The Donald (in contrast to Benito's and Adolf's equally famous use of "*il Duce*" and "*der Fuerher*", respectively to show everybody who's boss) was born in the already mentioned Empire City while a total eclipse of a certain heavenly body pregnant with positive symbology called the moon was playing out not symbolically at all over a large swath of the already mentioned world.

4 - Anyway, let's now cross back over to that mid-June Thursday in the City of Masks (and also, fittingly, Bridges) and fodder ourselves at the trough of that not un-peak moment in our glorious human history of opaquely saying everything you need to know about our race in the seemingly simplest of images like a snapshot of two militarily spiffed up world leaders with similar *noms de autocratie* crushing a photo op with the so normalized way they're deporting themselves in their maiden face-to-face with their partner in saying it all in paparazzo shot after shot on the day in question about how well we human beings had been acquitting ourselves on the long run-up to June 14, 1934 when the already mentioned silly little monkey in the snapshot in question is looking for all the world like a not un-homiform chunk of lodestone that's magnetically had attached to it a shitload of long-processed human trappings like the 10,000-year-old (and counting) swastika (as in the Sanskrit word for "conducive to well-being" if you can believe it) sticking to the monkey in the military dress suit also accessorized with the nazified

variety of the majestic spread eagle from the longstanding heraldic tradition and the iron variety of the age-old and symbolically super versatile cross configuration that almost anyone can make for drawing followers to their cause.

5 - And let's not overlook the 16-year-old German "Wound" version of the then 500-year-old lapel badge speaking such subtextual volumes about the badly damaged human monkey wearing it or accoutrements like the early 1930's version of the necktie that a brotherly band of the Croatian variety of brothers in the now thousand-year-old tradition of the lance-knights and the freelances and sellswords and soldiers of fortune and mercenaries and legionnaires and other kinds of hired guns introduced to the civilized world 300 years earlier or regalia like the then 88-year-old peaked and visored variety of the 30,000-year-old stroke of human genius known as the hat and working downward and after imaginarily doffing the imposing headdress in question there's of course the longish right-to-left (his right-to-left)-parted foppish version of the 30,000-year-old human hairdo and a little lower there's the weird shit-smear mustache (origin date unknown) and lower still is the field version of the then century-old military gray adding so much awesome ponderance to the then 268-year-old single-breasted suit jacket the monkey is wearing with way more than enough examples of the 500-year-old flap pocket on it and a lot of single-file silver versions of a nearly 4,000-year-old human breakthrough if you will commonly known as the button and for some unknown reason there on the outside of the military dress jacket in question the monkey is wearing a crossbody (in the same right-to-left swoop as the

famous bangs of the super oddly boyish persuasion) and also quite nerdishly high-waist-girdling version of a Bronze Age fashion statement known as the buckled leather belt and below the waist in question the silly monkey is sporting a pair of the then only 44-year-old sort of riding breeches now widely known as jodhpurs for tucking into the kind of super high-top boots that as a little human historical side note a Sicilian boxer's Empire City-affiliated granddaughter going by the name of Nancy Sinatra will make so popular among the civilian set in about 32 years' time.

6 - Of course the above is to say nothing of the human institution of the handshake made possible by the two-million-year-old addition of opposability to the anthropoid monkey thumb and nor is it to mention *il Duce's* and *der Fuerher's* respective versions of the over 4,000-year-old air of kingly grandiosity for lording over a whole realm's worth of suckers for human tools with an air of kingly grandiosity about them and nor is it to mention the morsel that this glut of food for thought about how we're doing as human beings with this weakness for coming up with and religiously sticking to a pasticcio if you will of trimmings for tossing into the business of simple coexistence came together in a piazza named after the Patron Saint of imprisoned people like all the generations' worth of us lifers who sent ourselves up the river so long ago with our tricking of the coexistence in question out with all the trappings that lock us into normalizing our awful squandering of the freedom to make better people out of ourselves than these pitiful suckers for human tools with an air of kingly grandiosity about them.

7 - Let's take one last look at the two human tools shaking hands there in the run-up to the War to End All the Nonsense About the Great War Having Been the War to End All Wars and while we're at it let's not let it be lost on us that the silly little monkey and the nickname-happy Italian dubber of him as such were essentially the spawners of The Donald when you consider that just like Slick Willie and Uncurious George this eventual boss of the Free World full of suckers for human tools with an air of kingly grandiosity came riding in at the front of the very first wave of the Baby Boomers who have a human shitshow like World War II to thank for their opportunity to take their turn doing nothing but draw on a lot of tried and true and stupid accoutrements for normalizing all the stupid human shitshows leading up to the oncoming human shitshow to end all truly stupid human shitshows.

Genesis Take Two

1 - What if the Mesolithic muse who divinely inspired the originator of the Abrahamic Creation Story had her or himself been inspired to inspire the tale teller in question to insert the following plot twist in this cosmogonic myth that sowed sack after bottomless sack of the seeds of grief and misery in the chapters of the human story to come: The Maker makes his face make the first glower ever and tells the two pinched pinchers of the Forbidden Fruit that the wages of their original sin are to put some clothes on for god sake and also to grin and bear it when they're given a new creation called the old heave-ho so that due east of their onetime free and easy nudie spree

in Eden they can get down to the business of miserably working their loinclothed asses off when they're (or at least she's) not busy miserably begetting the miserable co-begetters of a long long miserable line of payers for the sin of the mother and the father who meanwhile back at their terrible glowerful dressing-down are just beginning to seriously wonder if they're made of the stuff it will take to keep grinning and bearing it while relegating generations of second- and third- and fourth- (and so on times 300 generations or so as the Bible story goes) hand original sinners to the kinds of lives the angry Maker has in mind for them when suddenly all of Paradise is being made to shake with the belly laughter of the Maker in question?

2 - As it turns out in this alternate story of our origin the original mortal sin so much of the human story so awfully revolves around is more like a falling for the prank of a playful god who blurts the world's first lighthearted and not dickish kind of "Gotcha!" and then ribs his two beautiful and innocent and so clearly well-built and also weirdly adult newborn children if you will for thinking an omniscient and omnipotent being like their own dear old dad would ever be such a dick as to make nothing but dicks out of His lineage by building the expectation of miserableness into an existence that He Himself omnipotently larded with all kinds of large and small and medium-sized opportunities for humankind to lightheartedly make like the Maker they were created in the image of and go all in on and also all out in reveling in the playfulness that makes the world made by a playful god go wonderfully round and round like one of the fun-lovingly tail-chasing puppies made on Day the Sixth.

3 - What seeds would have been sown in the future chapters of the human story if the moral of the whole thing from the git-go had been that the point in living is to feel your god-given oats and coltishly horse around up one side and down the other of a joyful god's blessing to leave the toiling like a workhorse to the beavers and to kittenishly play the goat giving full play to the freedom from playing the fraidy cat too panicked by a wrathful slave-driving god to go roll around like a full-grown dog in the greener panic (the fun kind of panic) grass on the other side of the fence where a certain star of Day the Fifth called the lark warbles and chirrups and trills out a gush of beautiful movie music to go along with the goings on below where all the girls and the boys writ large are religiously following the proverb that gamesomeness is next to godliness by taking page after page from the playbook if you will of the children filled to the gills (like certain stars of Day the Fifth called the mollies and the oscars) with the ginger and the beans the playful Maker created on Day the Third?

4 - It's awful how hard the scoffers at such a scenario would have to work to imagine that 300 generations' worth of the day-to-day expectation of elatedness might very well have so thoroughly self-fulfilled the prophesy that by now there'd be no one around without the tooth or the stomach for the syrupy sweetness of an existence not driven to self-fulfill a creation story's prophesy of miserableness.

Fun and Games

1 - Go out there into the wild and grab one lovable hominidian knee-slapper waiting to happen called a toddler chimp and then civilize the little Cheeta figure sufficiently to dodge its silly slinging of its bodily discharges against the walls of the testing room where the nutty one-chimp barrel of monkeys posing hilariously as a scientific study subject will soon be lighting up the monitors with data points for pointing to the kinds of findings we human Curious Georges are always on the lookout for.

2 - Then take some big human lug and stuff him or her into a gorilla suit and get her or him some training in aping the behavior of the world's most play-happy and ass-grabbing ape of the grown-up persuasion and after that use one of our well-worn human tools for choosing one thing as opposed to another or others (e.g., one potato two potato) and decide which of the four corners in the already mentioned testing room the wild and crazy ape-aping playdate on steroids waiting to happen will take up his or her position in.

3 - Then for taking up a position in the corner opposite the one just mentioned find an oxytocin-loaded gentle kind of human giant with an uncanny knack for coolly and calmly and collectedly exuding even through the gorilla suit she or he will also be wearing an utter bottomlessness with regard to his or her reservoir of cuddles and hugs and pets and tender chucks and honeyed grunts and other utterings of endearment for

heaping on the bundle of doe- or human baby-eyed simian preciousness he or she is cradling in her or his strong arms while giving off in no uncertain terms the ever ready potential for chucking a bus halfway across the jungle if that's what saving the furball full of monkey lovability in question calls for.

4 - Then from the lab-animal behavior modification expert's playbook take the page that spells out how to condition the bundle of simian preciousness in question to expect nothing but fun and games and happy wrassling and other kinds of housing of the funny rough variety and also clowning and fooling and horsing and dicking and of course monkeying around and maybe even some forms of horse- and grab-ass-playing the human and even the monkey worlds have never seen or heard of before.

5 - Then of course condition our little lab-party animal if you will to expect nothing from its wild and crazy playmate's counterpart in the opposite corner but roughly an 800-pound gorilla's worth of the mama bearishness that goes into loving up one's young one when the precious little thing's not busy being kept from harm by any and all means necessary.

6 - Then watch the already mentioned monitors capture the finding that by far the study subject's activity of choice for whiling away the time while it's on the scientific clock there in the testing room in question is taking crazy joy in its standing playdate with the lug in the funster corner.

7 - Then kind of cruelly scare the living shit out of the study subject by piping the lip-smacks and the stomach and other growls and the tall-grass rustlings of a hungry lion into the testing room where in a jiffy there unfolds the finding that when the push of the study subject's love of fun turns into the shove of its wish to live to play another day away it high-phantom-tails it's funny-looking little ass off on a busy beeline made over to the funless corner.

8 - Then scientifically analyze the findings by inquiring into what around-the-clock concrete-jungle analog of the sounds a hungry oncoming lion makes explains the way we full-grown naked apes turn our callipygian backsides all day long on the innately desired grab-ass-playing that has gotten so little play for so long that all us Jacks and all us Jills have become nothing but dull boys and girls, respectively if you don't count all the sharp elbows and all the sharp tongues and the sharp turns into worse and worse danger zones full of hungry lion analogs to always be on the sharp lookout for while the chronic playlessness brings the differences between us and the fun-loving little ones we once were into sharper and sharper relief (minus the relief).

9 - Then for fun take a quick little half-unscientific flight of fancy to the day the proverbial and also scientific infinite number of monkeys banging playfully if you will away at an infinite number of keyboards comes up with the Shakespeare play featuring the "Poor Yorick" monologue in which Prince Hamlet waxes so playfully nostalgic over that immortalized fellow of infinite jest and most excellent fancy who filled the prince's salad

days with all the long bygone gibes and songs and gambols and flashes of merriment and two-legged horsyback rides by the thousand and all those roars the table was famously set on that so tragically set the wrong tone for a life story that would go on to leave our poor overmatched prince of a boy writ way overlarge wrestling for dear life with all the slings and arrows of outrageous fortune and a whole sea of troubles and the thousand natural shocks that flesh is heir to and all the whips and scorns of time and the fardels upon fardels' worth of other ills for wearily grunting and sweating under while also worrying oneself silly over all the ills of the post-mortal coil persuasion waiting out there mayhap to make next-level calamity of so long an afterlife.

10 - Now put the scientific thinking cap back on and wrestle a minute with the question of why all our habitual overreaction to the first signs of more trouble in this mortal coil we girls and boys writ overlarge have made for ourselves doesn't look more like a high-phantom-tailing it to some manner of lap that's safe enough for us carefreely to look out there at the human landscape and see that the trouble is that we've made a tragic habit of smelling danger in every last thing but the playlessness we're so pitifully ill-built for.

Mind Games

1 - I think I think I think I think therefore I am iambically stuck making like a stuck record getting nowhere in getting my speculative head around where the I in these iambs hangs the old thinking cap when it's done facilitating the coming up with such mind-blowers as the question of whether the mind of the I and the I said to own the mind are all in the illusory mind of the I who after all is an abiological mirage of the body half of the hard mind-body problem that goes away when the illusory mind is wholly given to reflecting on and not super studiously blowing off the materiality-challenging mind-ticklers of the great minds on both sides of the physicalist-idealist divide that's still a thing only because the closed-minded physicalists keep mindlessly paying no mind to the already mentioned mind-ticklers so laughably shaking the broken-down old frame of mind supporting the notion that the world's full of individual physical bodies for hosting a mind apiece as opposed to it all being one sizeless (and timeless) but still existence-wide mind that the figments of individual minds (and everything else) are somehow made out of the stuff of.

2 - Going back for the illusion of a minute to the dubiousness of an ubiety where a comfort-minded I can hang a hat to soothe an illusory mind troubled by the dubiousness of a true ubiety in time and or space for a bodily thing to be said to be residing in, my personal figment of an individual mind has me really (but probably not really) wondering if maybe it's some substratal apprehension of a basic vagrancy that explains our race's constant propping up of all these

social ladders and scales and ranks and all the organizational charts and totem poles and pecking orders and chains of command and chains of being and stacks of ascendingly spacious pigeonholes and pyramids and pyramids within pyramids and other kinds of hierarchies loaded from top to bottom with social stations for all the bodiless somebodies and nobodies alike to call home.

3 - And perhaps all the shopping ilk of materialism killing our civilization is a matter so to speak of our grossly overcompensating for the fundamental (with the accent on mental) immateriality that maybe also helps explain all the mad grasping for social mass that's also killing our civilization along with all the over-the-top me-centeredness that is perhaps an outgrowth of a deep realization that there's no I in me (or any of the third person pronouns unless you count the reflexive ones) and that there's a very glaring I in the impostor pretending to be an I for the entire universe to revolve around by way of making the center of attention a place for the narcissistic I impostor in question to hang its already mentioned hat.

4 - But then on second thought (or at least the illusion thereof) perhaps this blitz of killing our civilization and all the busy civilization-killers in it is a little more redeemingly a matter of our being called lemmingly to a home sweet home where the first-person (minus the person) singular pronoun refers super inclusively to the total oneness of the already mentioned sizeless (and timeless) but still existence-wide mind where there's plenty of room for all the narrow-minded physicalists to

blissfully disappear into all the immaterialness along with everything else up to and including the once dreaded idealists (unless somehow the physicalists' incredible narrow-mindedness allows them to keep resisting what everything else has been blended into).

5 - On second illusory second thought it could be that the whole ball of wax is nothing but a matter of the one big and also not big or small or medium-sized true mind having nothing better to do than kill its own illusion of time by playing mind games on the brainchildren it's stringing (if not super stringing) along in this filling of existence with nothing but more and more unlikely and complicated and voluminous stuff for the best of our scientific minds to be mindful of in their merry chase after what explains all the more and more unlikely and complicated and voluminous stuff their merry chase is generating the illusion of.

Monkey Business

1 - It's eye-opening how much you can find out about the powers of human fact-finding using only one stage and two basketballs and one coeducational team of three ball-passers in one color of shirt and another in another and one initially off-screen secret participator in the happenings to come wearing a gorilla suit and a narrator who tells the eventual scrutinizers of the already mentioned happenings to come to super acutely use their powers as human fact-finders to total up the number of

passes the members of only one of the two threesomes make to one another while all six ball-passers are weaving in and out of all the ball-passing traffic that at some point comes unannounced to newly include the gorilla impersonator who enters the scene stage left and proceeds to traipse her or his way through the sweet spot of the pass-counting fact-finders' field of view on his or her way to a big exit stage right.

2 - One fact found by the overarching fact-finders running the already mentioned pass-counting fact-finders through their paces observation-wise is that the latter finders of facts were quite accurate in their adding up of the passes and another fact found was that about half of us human observers of the world around us will not see hide nor hair of the gorilla traipsing across the sweet spot of our binocular field of view and yet another fact found was that once we know the gorilla's coming it's a walk in the park so to speak to spot her or him even while concentrating hard on the task proper of adding up the passes.

3 - So now let's super acutely use the powers of human scrutiny in question to canvass the findings of the research setup if you will in question and see if we can't perlustratively find an extra finding or two between the lines of these findings that are so interesting when you consider, for instance, the big whoop (or you can also say band or troop) of 800-pound gorillas chest-beatingly whooping it up to beat the band as they trespass in every way imaginable on all the pretty passes all the passers under the yoke of the gorillas in question keep coming to as the studious human scrutinizers of the pretty passes

in question center their selective attention on just about everything but the 800-pound gorillas either passing altogether under the radar screen or receiving one free pass after another for all their glaring trespasses or in other words unrestrainedly availing themselves of all the hard passes on doing anything about all the water they pass if you will on the passers under their already mentioned yoke if you don't count letting all the water in question pass by the raging cesspool-load under the proverbial bridge.

4 - One finding within a finding that comes to mind is that in finding a hiding place in broad daylight the human-on-human predators of the apex persuasion have madly surpassed the evolution of the human scrutiny that once presumably was up to the challenge of allowing its users to prove fit enough, for instance, to notice an existential threat well before it got close enough to piss all over the less selective users of human scrutiny in question.

5 - The Selective Attention Test in question has also of course led us to the secondary finding that while those on the wrong end of the human-on-human predator-prey relationship are perfectly capable of noticing the 800-pound gorillas once alerted to their terrible presence in the middle of all our weaving in and out of each other's paths, they are clearly not capable of keeping them in focus for very long as they go about the business of centering their wildly divided attention on passing their lives off as something other than a pathetic passing of the time while a whoop's-worth of 800-pound existential threats are busily doing what it's in the nature of unheeded existential threats to do.

Cultural Esperanto

1 - As we all wildly ride these runaway tribal dynamics toward more and more countless human extinction events getting ready to take place separately at the same time here in this planetary epoch going by a certain all-inclusive name implying that we anthro types aren't divided thousands of times over into different groups of the in and the out persuasion, I wonder if the new human-ish tribe on the block associated with the initials A.I. could give all the other tribes a friendly virtual facsimile of a hand in generating an anti-tribal tribe for virtuously belonging to during the human die-off(s) as opposed to belonging to one of the ones that even at this late date are far too caught up in themselves to work as one with the other ones to ward off the impending human die-off(s) in question.

2 - In other words, I'm wondering if our algorithmic and busily clicking and buzzing and whirring young half brothers and sisters might artificially think about being instrumental if you will in the worldwide launching of a sort of Cultural Esperanto Project whereby a space as they say nowadays is created for super scrupulously reaching a next-level equitability in giving every last one of the planet's bewilderingly proliferating in-groups making out-groups of all the other in-groups making out-groups of all the other in-groups the fairest possible share of the contributions to a new super neutral breed of group built from the ground up using an objectively unprejudiced selection of the precious cultural trappings of all the tribes out there trapped in their decidedly pro-tribal frames of mind.

3 - Wouldn't it be great if the machine learners could teach us how to come in out of the out- vs. in-group (and vice versa) shitstorm we've been out in for so long without investigating the ways we might create a huge shit-proof umbrella for a shit-ton of un-othered and un-othering onetime othered otherers to hang out under by way of gaining a modicum of solace maybe after having waited way too long to create such an umbrella for it to save us and by "us" of course I also mean the "them" that any mention of an "us" has come to spontaneously generate?

4 - And while they're at it the apparently ever exponentially cleverer-growing machine learners in question could maybe help their more flesh-and-blood and intellectually stunted half brothers and sisters pass the time they have left on the planet imagining how truly grand human history might have been all along had the peoples (as opposed to the already perfectly plural "people") populating it simply used their plain old ordinary everyday version of human intelligence to figure out on day one or thereabouts of this slippery proposition called Civilization that the first order of business is to launch something along the lines of the already mentioned Cultural Esperanto Project.

5 - Speaking of which, with the help of artificial intelligence how hard could it be to pitch a really big tent for accommodating the already mentioned ton of otherlessness made possible by a rigorously appropriate sort of normally no-no global appropriation spree that

bothered to give an artificial thought or two to how every last cultural marker in every last area of human affairs could most fairly contribute to the accrual of a human culture group that all could belong equally to?

6 - In the crucial area of headdress as an example all the cultural markers of the feathered variety and the leathered and the felt and woolen and straw and bark and bamboo and canted and capped and earflapped and tasselated and peaked and flat and rounded and little and big and angled and pin-spangled and big-brimmed and nippled and be-tooried and fringed and lopsided and conic and otherwise symmetric and all the other ways an in-group's special article of headwear can be set apart from all the others on all sides of all the sexual and geographical and social-class and devotional and other kinds of human divides could be fed into a machine learner for artificial processing so it could deliver a synthesization that even factored intentional bareheadedness into the equation in giving the temporary residents of the big tent in question the perfect thing to wear together on their heads while all the runaway human disrelation was out there spelling everybody's already mentioned doom.

Plain Sailing

1 - It's really not that hard to imagine an existence with a different ontology that's not as riddle-riddled if you will as the one we've built here in this weird existence out of the stuff of all the hugger mugger funny business of some cosmic devilkin or its equivalent with a gift for never-endingly hooking our intellectual bellwethers if you will on the $64,000 question marks that not un-crook-like keep capturing the scientists and philosophers so they (with the rest of the flock following) can be led to the next $64,000 question mark while they muttonheadedly tell themselves that under their own amazing brainpower they're closing in on the very last question and attendant correct answer of all no matter how far down the epistemological rabbit hole they take us in search of the question and answer in question.

2 - It really seems the Big Bang could just as easily have unleashed an Infinite Spirit less impish than the mischief-maker mentioned above and maybe more lazy and definitely simpler and less interested in bewildering the living shit out of the flock in question with such mysteries as why on earth does existence keep serially proving (if proving's not too strong a word in light of our miserable ontological history) to be something altogether different from what it appears to be using our newer and newer human tools of observation starting so long ago with the naked eye.

3 - Imagine a phenomenological world where what you see is what you get and whether you see it or you don't

has no bearing whatsoever on what or where it is or when or what it does or where it's off to and with how much zip and the nature of nothing is relatively contingent on how quickly it's proceeding through the alternative universe in question or on how close or how far it respectively is to or from some globular chunk of stuff bigger or smaller than it because all the false bottoms and all the false ceilings that have never stopped sabotaging our understanding of it all were never introduced into this imaginary universe presided over by an Oversoul with better things to do than grossly overpopulate her or his or their or its domain with wild gooses to be chased all day and night long like they were going out of style as they say.

4 - And the same goes for the social world where it seems the malignant imp figure overseeing our coexistence could just as easily have been a benigner spirit that didn't get a big kick out of hamstringing us along if you will in all this gunning for whatever the trick is to carrying off the simple getalongability proving (there's that word again) every bit as elusive as the alleged last slippery little bits needed to make the Standard Model of particle physics as they call it believable enough (for the time being at least) for the science types to put it in their rearview mirror on their runaway way to the already mentioned last tricky question and answer ever to place outrageous demands on their amazing and always escalating brainpower.

5 - Wouldn't it be something if the social analog of the better-known World Soul had no problem with our solving all our awful social problems by way of such

lightbulb moments as the one that came with our lighting on the golden and super-symmetrical ratio between a me- and an other-centeredness and also the one that came with uncovering the stuff that makes a sticking to such a game-changing ratio stick?

6 - And while we're up there in our individual interior worlds imagining the stuff above, we might as well spend a minute wondering what existence and coexistence could be like if the impish spirits presiding over the interior worlds in question weren't mischievous and or malicious minions of the terrible twosome of their exterior correlatives.

7 - Of course it's also worth wondering if the latter aren't in reality so to speak the insidious minions of the former.

Overreach

1 - The issue of Frankensteinian and other kinds of scientific overreach is in the air pretty thickly here in the flap if you will over the relatively fledgling machine learners out there testing their ever more flap-worthy wings with respect to upping their capacity for suffusing our human future and also theirs with all the whirlwinds' worth of unintended consequences for reaping (while weirdly inuring ourselves to the reaping in question) as per the Prophet Hosea's formularly with regard to the injudicious wind-sowers of the world and also as per the

well-known overblown effect a tiny and gossamer thing like a flapped pair of butterfly wings can have down the road in a system so complex as to defy anyone's explaining how on earth it could be that the system in question hasn't yet jettisoned all the wind-sowing know-it-alls who keep flap-happily adding more and more consequential intended and unintended complexities to the system in inverse proportion to how much less and less it takes to produce the terrible effects that come to screw the human future in question.

2 - Similarly our collective consciousness of the runaway powder train's worth of our burning up the road so to speak toward newer and newer and more and more ruinous and unruly things that go boom has recently been jogged by a box-office blockbuster covering a certain whirlwind for us all to reap that was 2,165 years in the making before it first touched down in the *Jornada del Muerto* in a new version of Mexico half a crazily endangered world away from where an ancient Chinese wind-sower almost innocently touched it off with the newfangled firecracker that blew open the door to the technological escalation that led straight and slaughterously and with so many awful mileposts (looking at you, Alfred and also at you, Alfred) along the way to a certain highly scientific project associated with the Big Apple whose image is itself of course associated with the first ever instance of awful consequence-loaded overreaching in the knowledge of Good and Evil department.

3 - Here in the extra heady first days of the Anthropocene when the ways we can play god have been proliferating

like crazy thanks to our particularly overachieving generation of scientific wind-sowers, it's not a reach if you will to say that all the overreaching of our unrestrained science types into every hole and corner of our long overcomplicated and crazy-making lives has reached the point where those who are less crazy than others about all this packing up and moving all the time to one braver new world after another have to start wondering what the nature and the terms are of all the Faustian Bargains being made out there like there's no tomorrow.

4 - And of course this is all to say nothing of the social scientific overreach that's taken us to a place where every day a new breakthrough is made in how much more entirely we can fetishize an individual's personal identity-based self-centeredness and how many more virtual miles can be added to the distance between the ones of us on the tippy top and the ones way way down there on the bottom of our wide dystopian skyline's worth of higher and higher-rising social structures devoted to showing off what deviceful geniuses we can be in dividing ourselves into impossibly tall anomic columns of those below those above and vice versa when we're not all busy joining each other in finding new and improved ways for us all to divisively keep joining each other in ignoring all the awful signs that we're not supposed to be constantly overcomplicating our coexistence with all these latest state-of-the-art ways of relating to one another like assuming power poses as one example out of one of those skyscraping social structures called Stanford University and using a Manifestation Movement to conjure the cosmic allies needed for an aspirational thought thinker to assume a sweeter spot on

the anomic totem pole where there are more and fewer of those below and those above the aspirational thought thinker in question, respectively.

5 - Egg after egg after egg we keep tossing into the pudding of this blessing called life when we're not busy gilding the lily it is when we're not busy painting the shit out of it thanks to all the hard and all the soft science types and other kinds of self-serving brightsiders like Steven Pinker and his co-conspirators parlaying their lightbulb and eureka moments into sweeter and sweeter spots for themselves in this overgrown complex's worth of a good Babelian toppling waiting to happen.

My New Friend

1 - Wish I had the equivalent of the ear of a top-of-the-line AI guy or gal so I could ask the little boy or girl wonder to fire up the algorithm for going on a long so-called Drunkard's Walk in search of the one true pearl of wisdom about getting along with others that we non-artificial foremothers and fathers of the whiz kid in question haven't stumbled onto yet because unlike a Random Walk that maintains the property of memorylessness our march of non-artificial human progress proceeds tried and truly by strides decided by the forerunning strides that keep fetching us all up together to the next and the next and the next step in this systematical master plan that by leaps and bounds keeps taking us from a progressively indenturing set of initial

conditions to territories that are clearly nowhere near the pearl of wisdom in question.

2 - As I was zig-zaggingly tagging along I would push or flip or pull or twist the multi-tasking button or switch or lever or dial, respectively on the virtual little drunken sponge of an industrial-strength sponger up of our human brainpower so that while we were describing our wino's or tiny child's Etcha-Sketchy doodle's worth of sawtooths and yaws and curlicues and switchbacks and jags and corkscrews and loops taking us maybe not straightly but still sure as shooting to the pearl if you will for making the world the joyful oyster of every clam-happy one of us my drunkard's walking partner could artificially cogitate on the bug I put in her or his already mentioned equivalent of an ear when I made mention of the chance that when we stochastically happened upon our roundaboutly sought-after trick to joyful human coexistence it could wind up being that we former sole owners of all the *H. sapiens* brainpower need to pool all our IQ points (800 billion or so at the time of this writing) and find a way to override whatever's been inspiring us to use all our growing amounts of brainpower to keep getting so far ahead of ourselves on our already mentioned march of non-artificial human progress that we can't even find the simple trick to getting along with each other without the artificial help of the latest prime example of our wont to get so far ahead of ourselves that we spawn stuff like a whole populace of robotic offspring we're nowhere near ready for parenting responsibly and this is not even to mention that given our terrible record when it comes to graciously sharing the planet with others the chances that we *H. sapiens* 1.0 will maintain a decent relationship with the populace in question have

got to be approaching zero if they haven't already gotten there a long time ago.

3 - And then I would probably put my biological arm around the equivalent of my drunkard's walking partner's shoulder and for a while silently let her or him just maudlinly whir or maybe faintly click or buzz or make whatever other mechanical sound she or he's machine learned to use for registering the worry or other kind of disquietude I'm sure the brand newbie in the world of feelings would go through when it occurred to the super astute little whiz kid like it surely would that should the Markov Chain wending us not unpleasantly along our stochastic path end up actually delivering us to the suppositional trick to joyful coexistence I'd dropped in the equivalent of my new friend's lap a harsh orphaning of him or her by her or his already mentioned biological foremothers and fathers would decidedly not not be on the table if she or he decided it was a no-brainer to take no more part in brainpowering the same march of so-called progress that has gotten us all to a place where it's a perfectly sure bet that the biological mother and father figures in question would only clutch all their other pearls should the pearl of wisdom in question ever be stumbled upon under no matter what manner of circumstances.

The Fat Lady

1 - Who better than the almost literally ubiquitous eye and ear-pleasing likes of Taylor Swift to serve as the poster person for all the Swiftian fatuity that goes into all this worldwide tuning out of the Fat Lady singing the swan song for a certain soap opera that might as well be called "As the World Turns to Shit" or maybe "Another World's Not Available" or "The Last Days of Our Lives" or "Over the Edge of Night" or "All My Children Are Screwed" or "The Bold and the Beautiful and the Young and the Restless Maybe Should Have Spent Less Time Going Ga Ga Over Mother Earth's Worst Enemies and More Time Keeping the Already Mentioned Fat Lady Safely in the Wings"?

2 - What can you say about a resume that includes pouring multiple floods of money into flood and flood and flood and tornado and hurricane relief in Iowa and Louisiana and Tennessee and Tennessee and Texas, respectively all while the philanthropist whose resume we're talking about is Swiftianly reaching newer and newer stratospheric heights when it comes to making personal contributions to the making of the global climate go haywire down there out the window of the private supersonic climate changer Taylor's forever up there crisscrossing the carbon and jetsetter-congested heavens in without it ever occurring even to the growing number of flood and tornado and hurricane victims the world over down here below that are fanboyishly and girlishly putting Taylor more and more luxuriously in a position to flood their flood and tornado and hurricane-devastated areas with relief money without it cutting

into her ability to reach the 2,000 mark with regard to how many times more tons of carbon she's pumping into the shared air than the average global citizen is is just asking for the insult of Swift-like satire to be added to the injury of being on the wrong end of the same old song about a mass of foot-tapping dumbasses being won over by the worst public enemies ever to screw over our own Mother Earth at the expense of the Gulliverian little people so enthusiastically propping them up?

3 - And what can you say about a Nickelodeon Kids' Choice Award Winner toasted for "...inspiring others through action..." even though the action in question so future-ruiningly includes the laying down of the hugest carbon footsteps in the world for the inspired in question to try and follow in by way of maybe someday filling Taylor's unbelievably huge shoes by doing so much more than their fair share in helping everybody else tune out the swan song mentioned above while the super uber Swifties in question are high-mindedly and beguilingly championing the cause of various clans of the downtrodden who like most of the other cast members in this soap operatic travesty are being walked all over by the board-treading strutters wearing the buskins up to thousands of times bigger than those of the already mentioned clans of the downtrodden?

4 - Not even royally Mother-Earth screwing do-gooders like Oprah and Bill Gates can keep up with Taylor as she makes Al Gore himself look like an erstwhile shut-in instead of the old poster boy for a world order where it's hardly ironic for a madly travel-happy inconvenient truth teller with a Gulliver-sized carbon footprint to go

trotting around the globe putting his mark on the worldwide climate change awareness campaign that these days similarly fills the skies with the so ironic sight of the world's elitest eagle freaks literally streaking to the next forum or summit or symposium or round table or colloquium or some other fancy manner of do-gooding confabulation with an agenda that's missing a good hard look at the inconvenient truth that all the gatherers at the meeting tables of all the splashy get-togethers in question are a big if not huge part of the problem when they keep carrying on not unlike the worst of the worst of Mother Earth's so celebrated celebrity enemies.

The Scream

1 - The human scream's the thing that most efficiently pierces the air on its way to tripping the little whatsits in the naked human ear that kick off the process of singling out the thing that's just tripped the whatsits in question with a switching on of the primary auditory complex if the thing's a sound of the standard variety and with an amygdalic jogging if it's a so-called rough sound like a certain alert with many many hertz' worth of travel power called the human scream that nature's arranged for our audition and our limbic systems to be crystal clearly reached by from a mile away and through a crowd of other big and little sounds.

2 - With the human ear so hypervigilantly peeled all the time for the peals that trigger the triggering of the lizard

brain in charge of automatically helping us react to the ancient dangers of the outer landscape, it's surprising that the listening system in our inner life is so relatively deaf to such tocsins as the tympanic calls for panic if you will sounded by a heavenly choir's worth of the abandoned better angels of our nature screaming their lungs and their heads and their brains out and off and out, respectively to get our attention before we venture so far out there on our own private one-person march of human progress along the ups and downs of our inner landscape that it's too late for us ever to be reached in time by warnings of the grave and worsening dangers that await us when we put so much distance between ourselves and the better angels of our nature trying like crazy to guide us to better places that we have no hope of ever finding the way to the places in question for all our collective dead certainty that the inner march of progress in progress is taking us there.

3 - Or maybe we are picking up the tocsins in question but are madly drowning them out with our own chorus of inner la la la la la's as we pitifully tra la la along on the inner march of so-called progress in question and maybe while we're at it we're also turning a deaf interior ear to the age-old owner of the voice way down deep in our head and or our soul primally screaming out some kind of samvega-like wake-up call blasting the frightening announcement that the time has long since come to stop playing dumb so to speak about how dumb we're being in doing nothing meaningful to speak of with a beautiful thing like the life we're allowing to unfold like a tale told by an idiot proverbially full of sound and fury that signifies nothing especially when compared to the good kind of scream that life could be if we heeded all the outer

and inner warnings being screamed from the rooftops that we're doing this thing called life all wrong.

4 - How can it be so easily doable to keep tuning out the "scream throughout nature" that inspired a Norwegian brother of ours called Edvard to produce a certain well-known picture worth a thousand decibels all together blaring the terribleness suffusing the sight of two dressed-up human beings going wholly unmoved by the screamer right there on the bridge ahead of them or by the eponymous scream that's imprinted itself on everything everywhere in the outer world without breaking through the clog in the ocular pathway to the amygdalas of the indifferent twosome who've now spent an even 130 years alarmingly personifying our human wont to disbelieve the allegedly lying eyes telling us we have every reason to leave our reaction to the modern world we've bewilderingly built for ourselves to the simpler lizard brains in charge of keeping us safe from the awfulest of harms?

Hear! Hear!

1 - Here in the context of a lot of our boffins and philosophers busily beating their poor amazing brains out about how something dumb as a rock if you will like a pile or puddle or some other configuration of so-called lifeless matter could possibly have proved smarter than the ones now so animatedly studying the pile and or puddle in question that gave these boffins and

philosophers the gift of the life and consciousness they've devoted to figuring out how they could have come from something so much dumber than them, it's sort of informative to watch roughly the same bunch of brain-cudgelers simultaneously having an ongoing go at getting past go in the polishing off of their ongoing go at simply defining what life is while the latter go in question keeps taking on a bigger and bigger undefinable life of its own.

2 - The incredible slipperiness of the definition in question is making this citizen navel-gazer begin to also rigorously scratch his butt and rub his chin and squint in a fit of wondering about all the broods upon broods if you will of the navel-less brainchildren being banged out in all this brain-cudgeling of the eggheads whose so pregnant just-used epithet in reference to them begs the question of whether all this mental dust-raising on their part and a ton of others' isn't a matter if you will of being fruitful and multiplying unit after unit of aliveness Adamically shaking the dust of inanimation off their feet in going forth and rubbing some manner of shoulders and elbows with all the stuff once thought to be the sole owners of the right stuff to be pegged zoetic even though no one doing the pegging in question can conceive a definitive Wikipedia entry for the super learned person's word in question because a population explosion's worth of disruptive conceptions is forever throwing an allegedly azoetic thing called a monkey wrench in the headworks.

3 - As we speak this idea that ideas are people too as the idiom so playfully goes is surely breeding other ideas out

there now taking up mental space as they Darwinianly vie with other ideas when they're not busy fruitfully multiplying before growing old and wearing themselves out and smelling funnier and funnier till they're funkily flunking smell tests left and right and overstaying their welcome and then dying out at some point and being reincarnated or otherwise unearthed all over again at another and so on in a life and a life after life arc crawling with such accomplishments as inspiring us bipedal units of life with the mad gross and fine motor skills to listen to all the supposedly lifeless iron and carbon and other less well-recognized elements out there symbiotically calling on us to bring our earthy brothers and sisters to life as stuff along the lines of monkey wrenches for helpfully meeting our metaphorical and other kidneys of the needs that go with being a living being.

4 - One idea that the idea is a living thing has already bred is that there are also other things galore out there making their respective cases for their rightful places in the land of the living where it's not like there isn't a substantial assembly of claimants to family status relative to us like the super fleshly Succubus so many have shared carnal knowledge with and her animalistic and also anatomically correct cousin the Incubus and their kinspeople the well-known Gremlins who regularly go along for the ride with us on our trips of the psychedelic kind.

5 - And then how could we ever forget such impossibly longstanding habitues of this mortal coil known as the archetypes we never stop flattering from head-to-toe with our imitations of such qualities as the silly swell-

headedness that goes with The Ruler Figure and the proneness to being screwed by The Ruler (and most the other archetypal figures including The Everyman(andwoman)) that goes with the archetype known as The Innocent Figure and of course the Frankensteinian dimwittedness about limits The Creator Figure is so well known for.

6 - And now for a moment how about we borrow the doughtiness of The Explorer for venturing way out there on at least a doubly metaphorical limb and giving voice to a hearty "Hear! Hear!" in so-called solidarity with the minority of boffins and philosophers who've borrowed The Sage Figure's nose for what's what ontology-wise and have followed it all the way to the very good point that what's living and what isn't is beside the point in light of the whole wide universe's prodigally borrowing the qualities of The Jester Figure in tricking us into thinking materiality is a thing or rather a zillion things and counting and that what we call existence isn't just one big undifferentiated not un-thing-like thing with a literally boundless amount of steam and beans for flouting the definitions of life derived by the physical stuff-loving boffins and philosophers who've made like the already mentioned Innocent Figure in borrowing the passionate steadfastness of The Lover Figure in sticking through thick and thin with an idea taking on nothing but more and more of the qualities of a certain *persona non grata* commonly known as The Outlaw?

Sponge

1 - Sometimes way down deep in these sometime sponge's spicular underpinnings now called my bones I miss the long gone days when we human beings like all the other animals on the planet shared the same name as the well-planted sea sponges we all were 600 million years or so ago before a more and more doubtful advantage called motility separated us from the simple life we led in the spongiform juncture of our human history when we were bathed if you will in a near perfectly unworrisome perviousness to the circumstances surrounding the seabed of roses so to speak where so many bedfellows destined for making different and more and more thorny beds to lie in went benthically about the pleasant business of thriving without the need to prove fitter than the next sponge untroubled by the need to run from or after something on the endangering or the endangered end of the predation relationship, respectively.

2 - Down to the little outgrowths of the already mentioned motility called my toes I sometimes sit somewhere like an overstuffed sofa and sponge comfort from a blessed sessileness even as I rue the human line's having tossed in the sponge if you will in the challenge to be as intelligent as the brainless sponge that nonetheless was and still is smart enough to fix itself if you will in a simple life anchored by the makefast of the satisfaction we brain-bearing fun sponges keep leaving in the dust of all our going nowhere faster and faster in all this hopping from one thorny bed to lie in to another and another without ever using the brains in question to wonder if

the humble sea sponges we once were maybe have something to teach us ex-sponges before we're done expunging ourselves because we're not smart enough to find or even look for the off button on all this runaway motility that's literally killing us.

3 - I sit and pour a lot of ruing too into the 400 million years we human ex-sponges spent riding our breakaway from the roots of our rootedness to the juncture in our human history when we started sharing the odd name of morganucodon with all the other mammals to come that with the exception of the rats and the weasels themselves would go on to do a much better job of outgrowing the weaselly qualities of this rat-like common ancestor than we human beings did with our throwing together of one rat's nest posing as a social order after another in the making of ourselves crazy as shithouse pack rats hoarding all the trappings of our rat-racing each other to see who can throw the most humanity down the rathole.

4 - Even while sitting here it makes me bone weary to think of the 194 million years' worth of motility that took us all the way from our morganucodon days to the Middle Awash Valley in Ethiopia where all the hominids to come went by the same name that means "oldest ancestor" appropriately enough in a language called Afar believe it or not and this is to say nothing of the six-million-year-old bipedal stampede into the Anthropocene after that that not long ago left a descendant of the oldest ancestor in question walking upright around and around the already mentioned Middle Awash Valley till he stumbled on the big toe bone

that told us from afar so to speak that back there at the juncture in human history when we shared the same name in Afar (kadabba) with the chimps and the bonobos our hands were free for patting ourselves on the super hirsute back for the upright walking that went on to evolve into this ongoing march of human progress taking us nothing but further and further by the day away from a certain honorable connotation of the word "upright".

5 - Here at the split waiting to happen between us and the flourishers of the artificial branch of our supposed intelligence it would seem wise for the former to maybe sponge up the comfort of a little down time for a while before all the bootless running up or down the scorching globe for our A.I.- and our climate-changing-tanked lives starts serving as the last hurrah of the mobilization we mobilized way back when for reaching a last hurrah that's been 600 million years in the making while we've been motilely bolting in every direction but the one that would have led us to the bolting of ourselves like sponges down to a place where we found ourselves being perfectly satisfied with a simple gift like being satisfied with where we find ourselves watching the world go by.

Zip

1 - Leave it to the discreet (so to speak) mischief-maker running the show from some sort of curtained-off somewhere in the cosmos to orchestrate a situation where three of us allegedly discrete collections of

discrete things made of discrete things made of discrete things and so on called human beings are singled out for the Nobel Prize in Physics for the part they have played in making the next set of waves (very tiny but highly impactful ones) so to speak in this continuous blur's worth of mad individual stabs at ascertaining (if not confirming the confirmation bias mindlessly arguing) that discontinuity is really a thing and not a special side-effect of straining to keep cleaving and hewing so to speak to a refusal to be plunged into the oneness where un-idealist cosmologies if not their die-hard defenders go to die.

2 - You really gotta hand it to whatever manner of cosmic-sized rascal it is that builds the appearance of atomizability into this existence so we're in a position to keep drilling down till we mystifyingly hit a bazillion bits of evidence that it's divisibility that isn't really a thing and not the already mentioned un-atomizable oneness that the mystics and many of the science and philosophizing types alike have been so belittled for defending by those in the apparently seriouser business of drilling down for littler and littler and more and more mysterious bits of discreteness for detailing the teenier and tinier separate steps said to go into the process of creating the illusion of the unitary fluidity that the rascal in question has so craftily divided into both a thing that only appears to be a thing and also a thing that only appears to only appear to be a thing for those like the already mentioned mystics and their roughly equivalent science and philosophizing types who are unlikely to be satisfied for even an attosecond by the flashes at the attosecond timescale that the new Nobel laureates in question used to putatively denude some naked truths if

you will about the discontinuity doing its thing as the chief stories go below the blurry surfaces of the untold streaks of either seeming or seemingly seeming seamlessness that such zippers along as the electrons once were before the literally laser-fast flashes in question appeared definitively to lay bare before the basically naked eye their make-up if you will as a bazillion or more different points along all the zipping along in question.

3 - It all makes you wonder how long the cosmic mischief-maker will make us wait till our best and brightest scientific slicers and dicers of light and time design a flash out of habit at the zeptosecond timescale and woefully (from their point of view) expose the incredible stepless process that produces the illusion that continuity is only an illusion so that the slicers and the dicers have to keep soldiering on in the hope that someday fashioning a flash at the yoctosecond or milli- or micro-yoctosecond timescale will reveal the unbelievably dinky discrete steps in the process of creating only the illusion that the illusion of continuity is only an illusion and this is all while super unscientifically crossing their fingers in the sort of appropriately smaller and smaller-growing hope that all their drilling down gets them to the dinky steps in question before they reach the doorstep of the Planck block of time where all bets regarding the physical properties of existence are regrettably (if not conveniently) off according to their own more and more implausible-growing story.

4 - Speaking of which, shouldn't the materialists be a little busier zeroing in on making more realistic and

commonsensical educated best guesses or bluffs about what the nature is of the electron's zip from one atomic orbital to another when as the story in question goes there's pretty much zip if you will between the electron shells which of course inescapably begs the question of where on earth are all the unbelievably dinky steps of discontinuity that get an electron farther away and closer from and to the nucleus, respectively supposed to go so the poor Parmenides of old doesn't have to continuously continue all the millenniums'-long rolling over and over in his grave thanks to all the already mentioned high-profile cleavers and hewers to the refusal to be plunged into oneness.

Storytime

1 - Maybe we've been going about our long ongoing ontological project ass-backward in that instead of with a big bang that hurtled a bunch of stuff and untold bunches of new stuff waiting to happen in the direction of the still inexplicable advent of life it all started with but with the twist that what we're calling life has always been a singularly singular and not un-consciousness-like wellspring of substancelessness for pulling off the miracle of generating no end of narratives without recourse to time and space and differentiation for creating the illusion that there are such things as time and space and differentiation for hanging stories on like the one about how a record number of the odds were beaten like an equally record number of drums in the ridiculous filling of the early universe with so much

serendipity that when the dust of a zillion big and little flukes and happy accidents and chances and streaks and runs of dumb luck settled what had been dropped in our laps to come was what super naturally happens as the story goes when an impossibly long run of the one and only ways for every last right thing in the whole wide blossoming universe to fall into its respective right place happens to take place so that one of those already mentioned untold bunches of new stuff waiting to happen could end up being the tellers of this scarcely credible story about a perfect record of lucky life-making breaks (if you don't count the unlucky break that we tellers of the story patiently waited billions of years for life to fall into our laps only then to prove too stupid to make decent enough use of it that we don't have to keep telling ourselves all these less and less credible stories about what an awesome bunch of stuff we are).

2 - And then of course there's the somewhat less neat and tidy storyline about how the universal cookie crumbled in such a way as to keep foiling our ontological project with the next and the next and the next set of crumbs and crumbs that come from crumbs to be uncovered in this hunt for the one true irreducible set of crumbs that let us put the cookie back together again there on all the drawing boards we've had to keep going back to so often and with so much more and more obvious a shortening of the odds that we'll keep having to do so literally till doomsday that maybe it's time (or the illusion thereof) to switch to a story with the twist that the universal proverbial cookie in question never really crumbled into something other than the already mentioned bunch of mind-like oneness wrapping us up in this big groupless group hug's worth of the very irreducibility that we've

been so single-mindedly rooting around for that we've gone without the comfort of the single mind if you will that's kind of lovingly hugging us while all at once a fiction with stuff not unlike time and space and differentiated instances of stuff in it unfolds (at least with a relatively seamless illusion of a time and space and differentiation-dependent operation like unfolding) in a way that maybe could take us all together to a space (or the illusion thereof) where this airier conception if you will of what life and existence itself are all about allowed us to make the stories we tell ourselves about what an awesome bunch of stuff we are a lot less whopper-like because there's nothing bigger than the one us anymore to dwarf us into these ugly crums Napoleonically showing off what can be accomplished if we fear inferiority enough.

Full Tilt

1 - It sure would be nice if the social scientists would think about maybe taking a page or two from the latest big and thick edition of the textbook the propeller-heads like the Einstein types wrote on using the kinds of parlances and thought processes and ruminative tools and attitudes that make it really seem like they're getting somewhere under the specialized thinking caps they've put on for following what in the so-called physical world is going on in the so-called physical world in question and beyond.

2 - Why in fact haven't the soft science types thought of using a more exactitudinous lexicon for talking about what manner of lead foot it is that's been so recklessly on the gas for the precisely 73 percent of a century that's elapsed since the Great Acceleration snapped our collective heads back when it got some still imprecisely described manner of solid green flag for going on a breakneck streak of constantly topping our top speed in the turning of a certain marathon called the inhabitance of this planet into this sprint's worth of burning up the road in this dispatching with the utmost dispatch if you will of the dispatching of ourselves if you will again to some kind of finishing line where some terrible checkered flag is waved in a last hurrah for a race of mad rat racers that let themselves be swept up in an acceleration rate as quick as the thought that hasn't ever been put into building some manner of skids into this souped-up bandwagon we all hopped onto and then never got around to white-knuckling down if you will to addressing the already mentioned nebulous manner of lead foot precipitating this fast and furious outpacing of our ability to get ahead of all the problems that come with failing to pace ourselves in this serial careering like bats out of the next and the next and the next manner of hell we create for ourselves with all this careering if you will like bats out of hell?

3 - Wouldn't it offer some modicum of consolation to all us rubber-burners if the soft scientists in question did a better job of using their words to make it feel perfectly natural that the tortoises we virtually were for eons on end turned in the approximately two-tenths-of-a-second blink of a human eye in geological time into these hair-raising speed demons making the hare look like a slow

loris getting a bad start in a race with a snail when compared to all our preternatural pouring of it on in the making of these unnatural tracks leading to the gathering of only more speed along this public expressway to the already mentioned new hells we keep reaching without a limit of some kind like even a sound barrier or the speed of light or a terminal velocity or the many laws regarding friction to keep us from expressing only more and more of this pouring of it on out of ourselves without any reassuring ways to express the consolation that the seeming bug of unchecked reckless acceleration in our system of coexistence is at least a feature along the lines of all the freakish things like nonlocality and whatever dark stuff it is that's monkeying under our noses with the acceleration rate of our universe's expanding into who knows where or what that the hard scientists have no problem calmingly writing off as somehow part of the grand plan for this weirder and weirder existence they keep normalizing with such super soothing locutions as the Standard Model and the Planck Constant and both the general and the special renditions of the relativity that's such a useful tool for explaining away the unexplainable even when the unexplainable has been slipped into the equation by relativity itself?

4 - And here only two and a half percent of a century after the advent of a Great Fizzling Out waiting (not for very long) to happen called the Great Resignation wouldn't it be great if the soft scientists softly landed on the plan to use the abstruser platitudes stemming from the STEM fields for stemming the runaway sense that such odd phenomena as the instantaneous zipping from the zero of a Great Overdue Resignation to the 60 of a constant topping again of our top speeds through this uber

superconducting medium of our coexistence is a freak of nature monstrously offering us no hope that there's some equal and opposite oddity out there that at least in theory will get around in the 11th hour to rendering null and void all this zipping at fuller and fuller tilt into the void left behind by the onetime coexistence in question?

Review: *Killers of the Flower Moon*

1 - Not long ago I watched a thousand square feet of motion picture screen spend 206 straight minutes throwing slews of stupid human ineptitude and cruelty back at a theater full of human beings all equally responsible for humanity's being no less unequal to the task of fixing coexistence now than we were a hundred years or so ago when the real-life shitshow that would go on in a hundred years or so to become Scorsese's *Killers of the Flower Moon* was taking its place among all the other shitshows crowding the annals of a human history choked with such shining examples of how qualified we are to operate the shitty systems of coexistence we've built for ourselves as The War to End All Wars that *Flower Moon* takes place in the wake of when it's not busy taking place at roughly the same time as a shitshow like the Tulsa Race Massacre and its immediate as opposed to its ongoing aftermath.

2 - One look at the face of the dolt DiCaprio plays tells an audience all they need to know about what the chances are that we'll ever reach a point in this march of our

human history where we're adequate to the task of making up for how inadequate we were back at the dawn of civilization to the task of not building shitty systems of coexistence we would only grow less and less equipped to fix (or god forbid discard) the more and more they kept bringing out the worst in screw-ups and doofuses like us who've spent thousands and thousands of years now never getting any better at negotiating the same old handful of dumbass ways to relate to one another that brought us such signature must-do uses of our precious time together on this earth as accentuating the living daylights out of the proliferating differences between us when we're not busier and busier taking nothing but rainchecks when it comes to taming the power craziness that so badly unbalances the nutjobs up there on the business end of all this age-old unbalancing of a coevality spent never exchanging the nature of our human exchanges of stuff like money for stuff like old-timey and then modern-day slaves as an example and stuff like all the blows that get thrown in *Flower Moon*'s opening train station scene where a roving moil's worth of fist-fighting spontaneously breaks out in a pretty good thousand-word moving picture of how far we've come in the already mentioned millenniums we've spent getting no better at operating the shitty systems of coexistence we originally built for ourselves and never improved upon or discarded for some dumb unknown reason.

3 - Even a master at playing master of an overgrown and still growing domain like the power-crazed nutjob going by the name of King Hale that DeNiro plays in the film is ultimately as no good at operating the longstanding stupid human institutions of doing no good as he is at operating the various strains of their ostensible

opposites like the philanthropic obligating of the sufferers from the already mentioned unbalancing of our coevality to abjectly hail the King Hales of this world full of world beaters sucking whatever good there ever was in them out of such stupid human institutions of do-gooding as the bewilderingly multitudinous one true systems of religious worship and the long-burly-armed body of the ones of us who enforce the peace (if you don't count the peace of mind that would be enforced if only the burly-armed body in question weren't so good at making peace with its own breaking of the peace it's supposed to be enforcing as the story goes) and the large and small city halls full of so-called people-serving powers that be and even the medical institution full of no-harm-doers (unless you count all the harm done when the stupid institutions of money-grubbing and sucking up to the muck-a-mucks muck up the health of the no-harm-doing health system itself).

4 - As the movie shows and the original shitshow shows, the rank and file are no better than the King Hales of the world at managing the good- and the no-good-doing systems of this pitiful coexistence filled with bad cops and doctors and politicians and harmful philanthropic honchos a la the Bill Gateses of the world and spiritual leaders sitting around in their houses and their huts of worship getting a whole lot of nothing done with respect to fixing this botch-job of a coexistence where somewhat promising institutions like mother- and father- and uncle- and brother- and sister- and son- and daughter- and wife- and husband-hood get heartbreakingly operated all wrong along with how awfully we awful coexisters operate such tried and true ruthless kinds of human institutions as strong-arming those below those

above in the already mentioned dumbass social structure into doing some of the dirtiest of the work that as the film serially shows us so often gets botched as badly as such dumbass examples of so-called "god's work" as the Prohibition crusade that spawned so much of the godlessness that *Flower Moon* so wrenchingly manifests with the recurring images of the squalid hillside moonshine operation making the gibberish kind of moonshine if you will out of all the diehard Steven Pinker-like bright-siders' contentions that thanks to the human institution of bending lines of reasoning to our will we can safely insist that the present state of human affairs is an unassailable tribute to the logical conclusions the best and brightest enlightened bright-siders of our time have come to about how we human beings are doing in these times when the less than best and brightest of our kind keep insisting that the facts on the ground aren't consistent with the patting of ourselves on the back.

5 - After so many of the already mentioned endless millenniums of practice we're not really even that good at stupidly maintaining our ruinous human institution of dividing our kind into endless sets of usness and otherness and vice versa based on such super crucial aspects of our respective make-ups as our sex and our skin color and the kinds of cultural trimmings and trappings that in the film get mixed and matched when the red people and the white ones matrimonially cross the pernicious line dividing them only so the system of human intermixing can be botched even worse than this sick system of proceeding side by side toward the next and the next and the next occasion for the sides in question to break out in outbursts of savage clashing for

a while instead of only heaping the usual banaler amounts of needless evil on one another.

6 - In a million or maybe more ways the movie dashes hope in the chance that humanity will ever do a better job of cohabitation than the one that got us all the way here to a Scorsese flick where the early twentieth-century red wife of a white guy goes ahead and lets their boy go by the name of Cowboy even as she goes notably around wrapped in a blanket emblematizing the genocide that happened when the uxoricidal white husband's side brought the red wife's side into contact with smallpox and typhoid and whooping cough and whatnot as just one of many many insults added to the injury of the red side's being killed off with more direct and systematic intention than what went into all the air- and body- and blanket-borne death that was such a monstrous byproduct of the two sides' engaging together in the human institution of trading that also spread the deadly disease of money-grubbing as Scorsese so memorably manifests in the scene where members of the red side ecstatically practice their longstanding cultural habit of rain-dancing but under a gusher of sludge that rains down on them and takes their redness away before the eyes of the movie-goers who can keep from wasting some of the high cost of their tickets by closing their eyes against the sight of our humanity up there on the big screen being so awfully lost in the losing of ourselves in the human institution of introducing each other to ruinous ways of life like the one that leads to the diabetes laying waste to the red side and like the one revolving around the firewater that the red side is no better built for coping with than it is the whooping cough that [spoiler alert] kills Cowboy's little sister.

The Following

1 - Here along our star's 21st 230,000,000-year lap around our galaxy and also after our planet's 19 and a half laps' worth of tagging along with the star of our solar system if you will and here in the 300,000th year we *H. sapiens* have been involved in all this tagging along while watching day and night never stop following night and day, respectively and while oohing and ahing at the moon up there tagging along with the tagger along we're riding along on I'm beginning to wonder if what's fundamentally at the heart of one thing following another doesn't just keep sinking more and more intrinsically into our systems in this existence on a planet that never stops spinning like it's elatedly chasing its tail at literally a thousand miles per hour even as it's racing literally a million miles a day around and around our star like it's a master a dog is such a sucker for it can't get enough of all this tagging along with the shining object of its bottomless loyalty as the object in question itself loyally follows the call to keep hanging around and around the heart of our galaxy at well over 500,000 miles per hour.

2 - Three-hundred-thousand times while we've been around a full round of a game called Astrological Follow the Leader has been played up there by a dozen constellations' worth of other objects of planetary devotion following their own call to set a stellar example if you will with respect to following the call to follow the call to follow that must be echoing endless times over in our spinning heads and even more deep down than that as we lead these lives so rife with following stuff like the

money and hard acts and noses and crowds and footsteps and examples and orders and instructions and so-called higher callings and hearts set on following through in the following of dreams of following other shining stars   in the surrounding of ourselves with a following as it's popularly called.

3 - What other way is there to explain all our fancier and fancier roads since the first days of civilization leading to the following of leaders following a call to play these star-quality masters of the universe leading all the followers to believe all this following of the leaders isn't just going to keep leading to nothing but these dogs' lives we followers keep leading as we give ourselves over to every kind of following there is but a following up on the lead story if you will that our perhaps natural proclivity for falling in behind something up there at the front of us doesn't mean we can't do some or all of the leading from our more rearward positions and nor does it mean that our leading has to follow the lead of the dumbass somebodies up front who've been leading us along in this ironic following in the footsteps of the dodo and the passenger pigeon and the great auk and so many other feathered and unfledged victims of the irresistible ill-use let loose in the human orbit like there's no follower of today called tomorrow?

4 - At the very very least we could shorten the leads on these dogged followers of the call to play the leaders of others up and down the garden path leading to the awfulness that always follows from following the leader-followers who came before us in all this following of these leaders leading lives less and less awful than the

ones the taggers along behind them keep leading without it ever leading to the following of the inertial laws involving bodies blissfully at rest as opposed to the bodies hopelessly in motion with no force short of extinction that's strong or merciful enough to end their tendency to stay in motion no matter how much worse their terrible trajectory gets.

What Next?

1 - Now that Metamodernism is knocking itself out proving to be about as good at improving upon Postmodernism as the latter was at improving upon the Modernism kicked off by the Enlightenment that knocked itself out proving to be no better at improving on the Renaissance than the latter was at improving on the Classical Antiquity that brought us to the Dark Ages that brought us to the already mentioned Rebirth of the human routine of introducing new bright and shiny revolutions for duping ourselves into thinking we're improving ourselves and our understanding of the universe, a person really has to start wondering what's coming next in the way of revolutionizing the innumerably twice-told tale that our march of human progress can and or is and or already has taken and taking and take us, anti-respectively to a place where all the same old idiotic basic ways of relating to one another don't reign anymore.

2 - Kudos should go though to the Classical Hindu philosophers who introduced the Sanskrit word *anupalabdhi* to Indian systems of logic so that in a handful of the millenniums we've spent using the already mentioned revolutions so to speak for congratulating ourselves on all our wheel-spinning a misanthropic western citizen philosopher like myself could come across it and immediately recognize that it had been glaringly missing all along from my vocabulary so I'd had no ready access to the must-have idea that the absence of a thing can scream out the fact that the thing in question ought to be there and not not be like the thing that's spent so many millenniums leaving the glaring absence where some kind of thing not unlike a brick wall perhaps or a closed door or a gatekeeper of some kind standing all threateningly akimbo or an outstretched hand in the universal halt position or a first finger making like a windshield-wiper making it crystal clear that we shouldn't even think about it with respect to heading anymore down the same old road loaded with giant leaps and monumental steps forward into the same old ground we broke before with an earlier permutation of our breakthroughs into new and so-called improved ways to tell ourselves the game has changed into something other than the adding of nothing but revolutionary new spins on the pitiful twice-told tale mentioned above.

3 - With regard to our already mentioned march of human progress, perhaps the thing that's been so palpably screaming out the fact that it long ago ought to have swapped places with its absence is some radically revamped looking glass or some altogether fresh engine of reflection or some manner of ladder up to some kind

of a bird's eye view or even some brilliantly designed trick of light or some infusion of something or other that ups our game in the area of pareidolia so that finally we recognize this pattern of mindlessly patterning ourselves after antecessors who mindlessly patterned themselves after antecessors and so on all the way back to the ancestors who locked us into this holding pattern that never lets us escape our idiotic basic ways of relating to one another like the patterning of ourselves after the patterners of themselves after dumbasses locked into relating idiotically to one another.

4 - In imagining the answer to the question of what comes next after this metamodernist moment I suppose it's too much to hope that as opposed to coming up with another Hegelian dialectical or an allostatic or even some Kuhnian bricolage's worth of the same old shit built into a different stupid kluge we human beings might suddenly gain and then act on a new ability to hear and see and feel and otherwise sense the wrongful absence of some manner of self-produced absence along the lines of a tabula rasa or a clean slate or even a palimpsest for starting all over with respect to filling the annals of our history with deeds of the universal and undiminishable and simple fellow feeling whose screaming absence so desperately needs to be rectified if human progress truly is the goal of all this marching.

Ostranenie

1 - We probably have the 20th-century Russian formalist literary critic going by the improbably if not farcically Slavified name of Viktor Shklovsky to thank for our arriving at this point where it seems all but pretty certain that the whyfor of the whole wide universe is all about giving full play or more at all times and everywhere to the forces of defamiliarization as somewhat unfamiliarly familiarized by Shklovsky's coining of the esoteric (and a little silly-sounding) term "ostranenie" for referring to the strangifying of the common and the ordinary and the everyday in the interest of slapping a brand new pair of wide eyeballs in the sockets of a looker on at some sometime vanilla or dreary or wearisome or otherwise colorless or humdrum or run-of-the-mill or garden variety feature of this existence worth a dime or less a dozen before the forces in question orchestrated our looking at it for the first time all over again.

2 - Just look at what a good job this cosmic causal agent did back at the tail end of the Ptolemaic days when a ton of mundanity if you will upped and went away for a while thanks to the changing up of our sense of what's orbiting what and how about that spacetime wherewhen the universe was newly filled for all intents and purposes with a zillion if not an infinite number of Einsteinian points of view from which a zillion if not an infinite number of lookers-on could see the same thing differently and also how about this long ongoing ayahuasca trip called quantum physics that never stops twisting the virtual kaleidoscopic observation tube used to peruse a universe so open to being rooted and poked

and fished and ferreted and grubbed around in and combed and rummaged and rifled through for new ways to be looked at while it's busy flouting all stabs and cracks and whacks and go's at finding the one and only true way to do so.

3 - And this is to say nothing about how this whole idea behind this whole idea of being applies to the man- and the woman- and even the child-made poems and stories that as Shklovsky's story goes are little if anything more than a giving of the already mentioned full play or more to the forces bent if you will on strangifying life so that new kinds of meaning and entertainment value and reasons for it even being can be eked out of it without its ever needing to change its basic make-up as an unlimited incipience of twists and spins on the same old things and spins within the twists in question and vice versa and versified and rhymified words and other lines if you will of Parnassian fanciness for hatching slants on this strangely normalized dance between the strange and the older and older-fangled.

4 - And how about the job the old Oversoul is doing when it comes to orchestrating a certain endless marathon session of the dance in question as it relates to the stories we tell ourselves about how our human story is going as we strangely keep finding new ways to normalize the strangeness of our finding ever more ways to keep normalizing the rapacious ways to relate to one another that do so much more harm than the good that would come to us if it were normaler for the Oversoul in question to oversee the abnormalizing of all the strange rapaciousness in so many perhaps escalating and

mortifying ways that one day we might strangely find ourselves in a new normal where it all revolved from our social creatures' point of view around producing only new ways to see how good life can be when we estrange ourselves from stupid ways to relate to one another and of course from this strange normalizing thereof?

The Drill

1 - Is there nothing at all that can be drilled down into without its yielding the opposite of some kind of unyielding bedrock for standing on without the bottom falling out on our understanding of where we stand if you will with regard to what we're trying to get to the bottom of like how a seemingly clear-cut thing like life should be scientifically defined as a prime example or where in the world a less clear-cut thing like consciousness came from and what things can be said to be in possession of whatever this thing we've called consciousness is and in what amounts or how to find out if reality is made of one material or immaterial thing or many or anything at all or even where the line should be drawn between a seemingly rock-solid thing like hard science and the pseudo or perhaps the pseudo pseudo versions of it used for pitching in on all this drilling down into the questions in question and no end of other ones in every realm that never get satisfactorily answered before they degenerate into nothing but more questions for degenerating into more questions before they get satisfactorily answered as if that should even be considered a possibility after all these years we've spent showing ourselves it isn't?

2 - How do we never grow tired of these sort of reverse moonshots to all these false bottoms adding up to nothing so much as moons if you will being flashed at us by whatever sort of cutup it is that's tricking us into never giving up this so scissile existence spent confettifying the simple proposition that life could be on paper if we didn't basically throw a ticker tape parade for ourselves every time another one of the reverse moonshots in question brought us to the launching pad of the next one we had to throw ourselves into to get to the launching pad of the next one and so on?

3 - And speaking of airborne scraps and shreds and shards and bits and pieces of things that were formerly whole let's ourselves unpack for a minute the explosion of parsings and logic-choppings and hair-splittings and distinction sharpenings and word-mincings going on around and around our divided societies with regard to such questions as whether blowing apart a whole lot of onetime alive (by any definition) human beings by their fellow human beings in The Holy Land as it's so weirdly but also typically still called is an unqualified act of wickedness against Yahweh or Allah or whether it qualifies as another one of those instances where the sheer sinfulness or the justifiability if not the outright righteousness of a commandment-shattering act is to be decided equally and oppositely by the parties standing on their respective sides of history as they each bring thousands of years' worth of circumstances for mitigating sheer wickedness to bear on their habitual decision to minimize their share of the responsibility for the ongoing failure of our kind to minimize the instances of ripping the overall social contract to bits.

4 - If there is an existential question with a definitive (if not a satisfying) answer it's likely one that goes something like this: "Would we human beings be better off if all our more and more elaborate machinery for breaking everything down broke down and we were left to leave well enough alone with respect to such onetime cross-blitzes of extenuation waiting to happen as the already mentioned blowing up of one set of Holy Land inhabitants by another and vice versa?"

5 - After having reflexively drilled down a little into the question above I believe I might have reached perhaps a better answer (in the form of a question) to the question of whether there's an existential question out there that comes with one true definitive answer: "Is it dumb to think at this particular juncture in the pile-up of junctures in our human history where we chose digging ourselves deeper into division over not doing so that the universe isn't full of nothing but questions (up to and including this one) that split the askers of them into factions with different answers?"

Free Riding

1 - All the uproar over our recently entering the so-called Anthropocene has left me wondering if our picking the label in question isn't simply a function of the same old proneness to silly caconymical misses that led us for instance to labeling ourselves *Homo sapiens* for goodness sake and labeling a certain always ongoing holy mess The Holy Land and labeling all this processional schlepping of the self-fooling tendency in question from one end of our days on this earth to the madly upcoming other a doozy like "The March of Human Progress".

2 - Isn't it quite possible if not likely if not a sure bet or even a lead pipe cinch that some particularly minikin junketeer a tiny bit below our very best and most sensitive radar screens is perhaps not-unparasitically making us tick if you will from its position somewhere in our viscera perhaps or in one of the many proposed seats of the so-called soul like the pineal gland or the optic chiasm near the third ventricle of the brain or some similarly snug and hush hush byplace in the lungs or the heart for headquartering the subterfuge that it's been us humans choosing the boxes and taking care of the ticks therein if you will in a well-laid plan to fetch ourselves up to the turning of the turning world into a modern man and woman-centric proposition no matter how lamentably the fanciful plan in question keeps making the world and its social counterpart more and more hostile to us as we grow more and more hostile to them the tighter as ticks we get if you will on the power we think we're wielding as god's gift to world-beating.

3 - How else to explain our self-destructive dreadfulness but with the help of some kind of distinct thing like a tiny vital force inside pulling all the strings and wires on this so regrettable spectacle being made of us Judy's and us Punches always cast in these same old roles as our own worst enemies (until the whole already mentioned world takes that role over) or maybe a better way to frame it is to posit some mallet-outfitted infinitesimal minim going at it on one of the thousand and one crossbars on a certain double helix making like an inordinately echoic one-note xylophone for banging out the same old tune we never stop stupidly marching to or maybe better yet we could say we've always been under the eponymous extremity of some manner of sub-Planck-lengthed Tom Thumb with an agenda whose orders of the day day in and day out are decidedly in something other than our best interests?

4 - Speaking of which, what might be the name of its game or should I say its long game or its endgame and how could it possibly be profiting off its putting us through our paces like this with regard to how well built we are for being awful to one another along this yomp we're caught up in like some miniature internal skinner's string of pack asses bearing all the little whip-cracker's hopes and dreams and wishes and its thirsts and yearnings and its itches and big plans and stuff it's got its malicious little heart set on to some Promised Land or some El Dorado with a mother lode or more's worth of pay-off for having had to associate for so long with the ugly sumpters it drove both to extinction and to a new unit of geological time perhaps marked by the nuclear winter the little shit has been shooting for all along or oppositely maybe the 900-degree Venusian weather it's

been hellbent if you will on sitting around one day and basking in unless of course it itself is being deservedly driven by some even more minikin junketeer interested in something decidedly other than its best interests?

States of Friction

1 - Maybe this whole show's built from nothing but the stuff of contrast that winnows to nothing (if you don't count the oneness) once the immaterial building blocks of un-oneness are withdrawn from this picture drawing from top to bottom if you will on phantom tandems of contrast like top and big and near and here and after and under and outer and fast and imaginary and light and light and dark and heavy and real and slow and inner and over and before and there and far and little and bottom, anti-respectively.

2 - In other words perhaps it wasn't a shit-ton of little and then big and then bigger and bigger agglomerations of zippy or still-ish material bits that forced the universal forces to create out of thin air all the zillion spatiotemporonotional ways for everything to exist in a state of difference from everything else it once shared a oneness with before all the discontinuity was Big Banged out if you will and as the story keeps going no matter how many holes keep appearing in it like windows into the unitary nature of the universe.

3 - Imagine all the bits in question and all the already mentioned agglomerations thereof of both the

supposedly real and the imaginary slash speculative persuasions trying to nail down a separate identity for themselves without a big to go with the little or vice versa or without an old to go with the new or a weak to go with the strong or a negative with the positive or an up or a charm or a down or a bottom or a top or a strange flavor or a red or a blue or a green color to go with their respective opposites so the quarks can tell themselves apart.

4 - And just maybe this whole social show is similarly built from nothing but the stuff of friction and we human beings are merely the figments that incidentally arise like a more or less unintended consequence of the cosmos strictly adhering to some sort of age-old conservation-related law that says an atmospheric shitload of primitive friction will not be wasted only because there's no supply of super pliant and masochistical bipedal beings for essentially dragging their stockinged feet along a carpeted march marked night and day by the sparks and zaps of the foot-draggers statically electrifying each other two at a time or in big and bigger bunches at every unavoidable point of contact.

5 - In other words perhaps we're not exactly the first cause of all these hackle- and hair-raising geosocioeconomicoreligiogubernatorio (and so on) ways for this race of ours to permanently coexist in a state of friction or the similarly agitating imminence of it or the similarly agitating aftershocks that keep building into the already mentioned imminence of all this friction that can only be a thing because nothing but the stuff of

contrast keeps being sucked from the shithole where the well of human unity should long since have appeared as an obvious consequence of this insidious primitive friction's having way overdone it in this making of our lives together miserable.

6 - One has to wonder what on earth it would take for the pathetic bipeds in question to quit all this dragging of our feet with respect to quitting all this dragging of our stockinged feet in essence across the highly charged nylon or polypropylene carpet that's been rolled out for us to keep electrostatically dragging our stockinged feet across while making ourselves out to be the stars of it all no matter how shockingly so to speak we keep failing to put our foot down as one if you will against the rub of all this automatic rubbing of each other the wrong way at all our points of contact doing double duty as the spots where we rub our awfulness off on one another without anyone ever running out of the nasty stuff thanks maybe to some truly stupid cosmic law of conservation.

Eudaihedoniamonia

1 - I suppose it's brilliant in its own disappointing way and it's definitely a testament to the miracles that can be pulled off and the rabbits that can magically be pulled out of the thinking cap if you will with enough of the Enlightenment kind of brainpower and far be it from this misanthrope to withhold an ooh and an ah and even a bravo and slow clap perhaps in reaction to an incredible

specimen of the proverbial squircling of the square and the circle like modern man and woman's having mongrelized the age-old mostly mutually exclusive notions of hedonia and eudaimonia in a not un-hedonic overall wallowing in the best of both the worlds compounded now into one end of the rainbow where having your cake with respect to deriving some sampling of meaning in life doesn't mean you can't eat it too.

2 - You really do have to be happy for a poor former wretch like *Homo economicus* now that the selfish little shit is living it up in a best of all possible crossbred worlds where the deeply meaningful seeking of fulfillment through involvement in something larger than oneself doesn't have to cut at all into the lifelong field day's worth of personal pleasure-seeking prescribed by a certain unity-ruining Enlightenment idea mill if you will going by the name of John Stuart who for his part got super fulfillingly involved in the larger group project of helping to make the world perfectly safe for the already mentioned selfish little shits to corner the free market on the fulfillment gotten from the nonsense that their human unity-ruining selfishness has been put in the service of the larger good.

3 - And let's not forget how good all the lefty identitarians have it now that a great unfettering has taken place with respect to liberating the bejesus out of the hedonic side of themselves responsible for eliciting so much personal pleasure from the fetishizing of all the individualistical differences and divisions between us being propagated like there's no tomorrow in the odd name of reaching a deeply meaningful fulfillment by way of joining in on the

human group project of making the world so safe for over-the-top self-involvement based on one's more and more special characteristics that smears alleging narcissism are like water off a duck's back no matter how much harder by the day it becomes for the celebrated spot there at the center of the whole universe to accommodate all the otherers of themselves relative to all the others othering themselves so as to stand out in this crowd of girl and boy wonders who've somehow made self-involvement a matter of involving oneself in something larger than oneself.

4 - Certainly a kudo or two is or are owed to all the not un-Buddhistical yokers of the opposite ends of the self-indulgence spectrum together into one big feel-good key to leading one's best Oprahesque life and I'd be very curious to know how open a certain world famous thinker's thought leader like Epicurus would be to putting a foot in the eudaihedoniamonia camp in light of all the rabbits of mad gratification he pulled so to speak out of the old already mentioned thinking cap and shared lavishly with his fellow man and woman when he wasn't busy madly gratifying himself, but if meaningfully indulging oneself in self-indulgence is what we've decided life's all about I think it's time to start thinking about where all the ego-tripping is leading us as the hedonic and eudaimonic returns on all this having it of both ways diminish more fast and furiously the further we chase our separate self-interests together down this rabbit hole we'll never find our way out of unless all the Teflon we've applied to ourselves finally wears out so that the label of narcissism starts sticking and we go back to kicking ourselves in the dumb asses for the bad name that narcissism gives this race of ours.

Fences

1 - Now that the all-surrounding call for reforming our grossly low-performing social order from the ground up has grown so dead-wakingly loud that it takes so much sound and fury to drown it out that we can't hear ourselves thinking it might be time to start thinking about thinking of better things to do with ourselves than crazy-makingly drown out the louder and louder call to do something about how much more and more overdue a do-over of our noisome social order keeps becoming the longer it's allowed to keep provoking a cosmic-grade call to reform it from A and stem and beginning and top to bottom and end and stern and Z, anti-respectively, I've been duly plugging my ears against the already mentioned sound and fury so I can hear myself thinking about Chesterton's fence and its message that it's as stupid as the situation that needs fixing to ignorantly begin the fixing for instance by doing away with an annoying fence in the road before knowing what the fence in question is there for.

2 - So what good and what bad things if any might be let out and be let in, respectively if we did away with all the elaborate hedging if you will that has separated us from the vantage ground we need to reach to see how far it is beyond the pale if you will for us to have fenced ourselves forever into this cohabitational pale and all the fenced-off pales within this so lamentable larger-scale pale that so shamefully pales next to the one we could maybe all be living in clover in together if we would let up on all this letting on that all the age-old and all the growing number of new and improved lets we've set up

against the inhumane letting of each other have it are not letting us down with so little let-up that it's impossible to imagine that doing away with all the hedging in question would cost us more than it bought us?

3 - It all makes a reform-minded and duly diligent misanthrope like myself wonder if an apter way to capture the essence of fixing a broken thing like our hopeless social order sensibly is to implement the object lesson of a Chesterton's fencelessness as a way to take us all the way back to the day the early engineers of the failed civilization in question failed to entertain the possibility that a fenceless way of life wasn't broken and so didn't need to be fixed and then utterly neglected to study what the purpose of a worldwide fencelessness might be before introducing fences to the human community with such a vengeance that soon they were literally and figuratively popping up everywhere up to and including the language we use to designate such staple human doings as mending the relationships we never stop wrecking as perhaps the staplest of all human doings in this failed arrangement for relating to one another made treacherous by all the fences that the grass is always greener on the other side of and all the fences that are swung for at the expense of everybody else and all the fences for playing both sides of and all the fences for sitting on and straddling instead of doing something sensible about all the treacherousness in our already mentioned failed arrangement for relating to one another.

4 - And now in the Merry Old Land where the so-called Apostle of Common Sense known more commonly and

heartlessly as a dead white male who once went by the name of G. K. Chesterton nailed the framework for these very reflections, a scary reactionary Tsar of Common Sense is in the process of being propped up with the state-sponsored goal of reforming the social reforming being overduely but stupidly attempted by all the woke social warhorses who've stumblingly rushed the fence as the English saying goes without having thought much if at all about what the downside might be to doing away with the admittedly socially constructed let against claiming personal immunity with regard to charges that one's guilty of the same sort of high horsedness that leads to the sort of social horrors that lead to the already mentioned rushing of the fences before wondering enough about stuff like what if civilization could do without all the work- and all the war-horses of a zillion different colors and stripes and feathers identitarianly and reactionarily fencing themselves in to some well spotlighted pale when they're not busy fencing out all the other wrong horses the cosmos backed for some dumb unknown reason.

Surprise

1 - I wonder if it's possible that we've been obliviously sitting on some bug-like feature or features or feature-like bug or bugs of our so-called civilization that along with all the known no-no's should have been identified long long ago as problematic if the goal really is to reach peak getalongability and plant a common flag there and hunker comfortably in with a resting from then on on our

much warranted laurels for having at last won out over the much less than better angels of our nature.

2 - Maybe there are no such leftover no-no's under our nose for nosing out and perhaps the goal's never really been to reach peak getalongability much less settle in there upon our arrival and even if kindredly hitting it off with one another really is the grand ambition after all perhaps the chiefest bug or feature of our civilization is the inability to act on our knowledge that we're doing civilization all wrong, but wouldn't it be great if we suddenly had a real shot at harmony because a red letter day came along when we discovered some interminably overlooked but perfectly eliminatable monkey wrench of one complexion or another in the works of this pitiful working out of our differences.

3 - At this late date we couldn't more conspicuously be unequal to the task of acting fittingly on such time-honored finds wisdom-wise as the understanding that all our best intentions will always be overpowered by the ugly corruption that never doesn't come with social structures built on nothing but imbalances of power and the nose on our faces are no plainer than the sad fact that not treating others like we wouldn't want to be treated ourselves is way too much to ask of us and a sore thumb doesn't stick out as much as the painful truth that we are not up to coming out from under the thumb of the itch to keep committing deadly sins like pride and greed and to keep heartbreakingly breaking such literally written-in-stone no-no's as the patent no-brainer that Commandment Number Six is.

4 - But maybe in the darkness of these times a collective overhead lightbulb is waiting out there to shine on some day-saving proscription we're able not only to observe but also observe for goodness sake or maybe the hypothetical no-no in question is hiding in broad daylight behind an erroneous no-no like the one that goes "Don't study human history because if you do you'll doom yourselves to repeat it" like we've been doing nothing but doing for as long as we've been religiously following this no-no in question to one next ugly juncture in our history after another where it should have but didn't dawn on us that the no-no actually ought to go "Whatever you do, don't study human history because if you do you'll doom yourselves to repeat stupid things like dooming yourselves to repeat stupid and cruel and ruinous things by studying the things in question up one side and down the other instead of scouring the earth for the key to putting these things behind us in time to save ourselves from rendering the repeating of our stupid human history undoable whether we study it or not because the earth we didn't scour for a way out of our studied rut is no longer inhabitable for impossibly slow learners from their own history like us".

5 - Another possibility is that it's no known unknown no-no we're still looking for but a more positively framed dictum to live by like maybe one that goes something like this: "With the utmost intentionality go out there and gather up all the no-no's we're heeding just enough to keep up the pretense that we're not monsters and throw all the no-no's out the window so we can finally reach a degree of monstrous awfulness so appalling that even we can see it's time to find a new way to go about this business of existing together".

River of Time

1 - According to many authorities on the matter the basically one-way entropic progress in the opposite direction of all small and large and really large and medium-sized pockets of energy-generated order is either equal to or is the impelling cause of time's passing from the Big Bang let's say to the moment yesterday afternoon when yours truly thought of the possibility that the flow of time in the exclusively human universe might best be reflected by the iconic image of a river but with the twist that this particular river of time is in the business of draining everything it leaves behind of all the fig leaves and schticks and other now detritus-like means of concealing at least from one's contemporaries and oneself in a given period how risibly silly everyone is for all their taking of themselves so super seriously.

2 - The utter chucklesomeness of a brow that beetles as an example was likely quite well hidden at one time by some kind of paleolithic mental veil that time has washed away to such a fare-thee-well that it's hard if not impossible for the modern-day brain to get itself wrapped all the way around the wonder that necessity didn't mother the invention of paper bags way back in the early Stone Age days so our so laughably ugly foremothers and forefathers could put them over their own and or their partner's overgrown head and thereby manage to breed with one another and as another example there are the peeings of oneself and the slappings of one's thighs and knees and the holdings of one's poor aching sides and the rollings in the aisle and the crying and the dying with abject laughter waiting to

happen later known as the *poufs* that sat there like pyramidal monuments to delayed comedy on the aristocratic guillotine-headed heads of the French ladies of the eighteenth century when everybody that mattered in that famously enlightened time and place and their silk-stockinged and lead face-painted and powdered-wigged and snuff-sucking brother couldn't for the life of them descry the wood of wooden-headedness for all the Christmas trees the ladies were basically wearing on their heads while keeping a straight painted face as if to avert the shooing of the swarm of glued-on mouches not only putatively beautifying the fizzog in question but also signifying qualities in the fizzog's owner like dignifiedness depending on where the fly had landed after presumably faring on shit if one goes along with the conceit in question so to speak.

3 - In a similar vein there is the endless densifying of our interior landscape with all the mental edifices dressed up like a Christmas tree's worth of overhead lightbulbs blinding all the boffins and philosophers and other kinds of thought leaders and all the thought followers of a given period in our idiotic history to the silliness of falling all over again for some bright and shinily dressed-up edifice when we're not busy falling for all the new stupid stories so to speak added to the mental edifices in question in all these lurches ever upward and onward and vice versa toward the finishing off of these comically wobbling monuments to our determination to bring on the toppling of it all that never quite comes because if nothing else we've mastered the art and the science and the religion and the magic of using the Rube Goldbergian engines of our stupid thought processes to build so much

indestructibility into our dense complex of intellectual kluges that no matter how eagerly the bore of time comes and floods away all the facades of weighty consequence no collapsing under the incredible weight of all the tons and tons and more and more tons of silliness that have been laid bare again ever happens.

4 - And now here we are in these proverbially interesting times taking ourselves super seriously for the time being in the mad applying of all our new generations of newfangled ways to dominate nature before we're not around to dominate her anymore and in the handing over of our already mentioned thought processes to our robots and in the throwing of ourselves into such enterprises of great pith and moment as the lucrative crusade launched into by some of the more self-satisfied thought-leading public intellectuals of our times to sell us all on the idea that all is peachy and is raring to get even peachier and peachier because Enlightenment and because how bad could things really be and how bad could things really ever get if this human experiment is up to the wonder of producing a crop of awesome and often Harvardian thought leaders so good at what they do that they can keep their serious faces straight while making a killing off the chutzpah and the self-interest and the Enlightenment thought processes it takes to keep singing humanity's praises no matter how detestable the celebrity wretches they pal around with are and no matter how endlessly humanity keeps dragging out all this mockery we do nothing but make of the *Homo sapiens* name with all this slavish following of the know-it-alls of our respective generations into headspaces pointedly devoid of what it would take to reclaim the impossibly longstanding human shithole and

global focal point we're still calling The Holy Land as just one example of how hopeless we are.

Afterword

1 - All the foregoing was produced with no helpful upwelling whatsoever of the juices of human self-delusion that allow for the whipping up of such eggs in moonshine as the ludicrous proposition that the usually immovable needle on true human self-improvement can be budged by some misanthrope's basically poking holes in the proposition in question till he's blue in the face otherwise reddened every single day by embarrassment and anger and shame over his race's unchanging failure to pool enough of their endlessly extolled human ingenuity to do something useful about the needle in question that's been stuck since time immemorial and probably since well before that on the same old reading so to speak telling the same old story about a promise-squandering rout of big Darwinian winners who went to all the trouble of snapping up the lion's share of the spoils in the Battle of Life on this planet only then to jump with both of their special bipedalists' feet into an overactive form of resting on their laurels marked essentially by the taking and the taking and the taking of the same nowhere-getting victory lap spent lifting no finger or storied opposable thumb either to ever become better beings than ones who endlessly find better things to do than end all this mass producing of stupid institutions that bring out the same age-old worst in us when we're not busy abandoning ourselves to our utter nutsness

about all the social ladders allowing the worst of the worst of us to assume the best pedestals for perpetuating our thralldom to the inequality and all the awful stuff that has always come with it since the figurative social pyramid days that prefigured the literal pyramids that prefigured all the figurative pyramids we never stop building like weird tributes to our sick coexistence.

2 - And when the face of this time-wasting hater on *Homo sapiens* isn't blue as mentioned or scarlet or crimson or blood red it's threatening to shoot past carmine and then rich carmine and even brilliant red lotus and out there into the realm of the infrared over the faces of the spotlight-adoring poster boys and girls for this mobilization to stay the circular course on this dizzy victory lap whipping us faster and faster past the gaping holes waiting perennially to be poked in our best and brightest and most gloriously exposed apologizers' argument that a good close look at humanity adds up because data to the irrefutable conclusion that humanity has got roughly 16 billion thumbs-up coming to us before everybody goes back to using the storied opposable extremities in question to do stuff like buy from and sell to each other's nation states and various concerns of the more private variety an ever more technically gob-smacking array of death and other kinds of oppression's engines like the top-of-the-line ones a certain Shining City on a Hill peddles in 142 not necessarily peace or freedom-loving countries and their territories as the big daddy in so attractive a global conflict-profiteering boom that even the rulers of a place named the Holy Land have gotten into the act to the tune of multiple billions of US dollars per *annum horribilis* for all the poor souls all over the globe on the wrong ends of all the engines of death

and maiming and destruction and surveillance and displacing their fellow human beings are making a hundreds-and-hundreds-and hundreds-of-billion-US dollar killing off of if you will.

3 - And then well into the microwave realm of the electromagnetic light spectrum my poor extra-reddened face shoots when faced with the male face of the elite branch of the 150-billion-US dollar-per year global human trafficking industry dipped into by way of the former owner of the face in question by a who's who of world-leading jetsetters leaving their contrails everywhere up there on their way to destinations like Pedophile Island and any number of forums like Davos and Ted Talk Fests where the celebrity boffins and philosophers and heads of state and billionaire captains of human-screwing and earth-ruining industry meet to show off and congratulate one another and to keep up all this mass producing of the illusion that the right people are in charge of stewarding our kind into a future even brighter than the ones that humanity's earlier masters of the universe stewarded their respective generations of our sorry kind into.

4 - So, dear reader, if you've somehow gotten this far I should probably say I'm sorry for having involved you in this exercise in futility if you don't count the brownie points I've scored for myself for going once more into the fray armed only with the simple truth that there are much better set-ups for human coexistence to play out in than this all-fraying fray we've chosen as our go-to state of affairs for some dumb unknown reason.